THE COAL SCAVENGER'S DAUGHTER

VICTORIAN ROMANCE

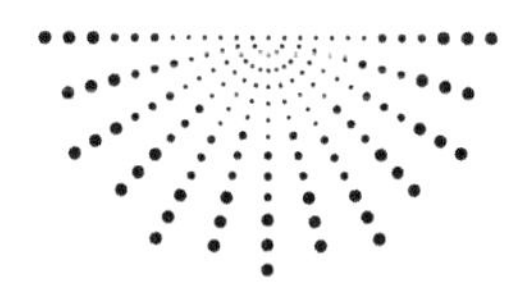

ROSIE SWAN

PUREREAD.COM

CONTENTS

CHAPTER ONE

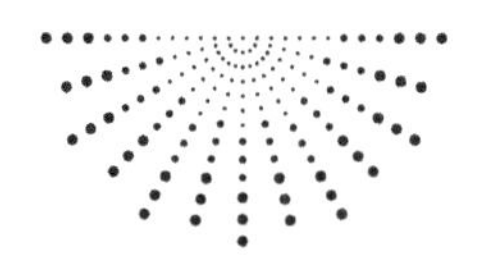

Sheffield, England, 1865

Milcah Fox, age nine and a half, was the oldest of seven children, with an eighth sibling on the way. Her father was a peasant farmer, and although her family owned its own little scrap of land in their village near Sheffield in the North of England, the half-acre had stubborn soil, and it barely produced enough to feed the family, let alone to sell. Her father made his money labouring on other people's land, while her mother did what laundry and mending she could find in their village, where the mine owners and businessmen were far outnumbered by poor miners and farmers.

The family could not afford to send any of the children to school, and so Milcah could neither read nor write, but she did not feel the lack of it. She would not have had time for schooling, anyway, when her daylight hours were split between taking care of her younger siblings while her mother worked or rested, and scavenging around the coal mines, searching for any dropped pieces of coal that the family might be able to sell.

It was a poverty-filled existence, but Milcah had never known anything different, and family life was so full of love and laughter that she was perfectly content with the little world that life had given her. Her mother worked hard to make their food stretch as far as it could, creating the most delicious meals from the humblest of ingredients. Her father toiled all day, but he always made it home before the children went to bed, so that he could hear all their jokes and news from the day and tell them another installment of his epic bedtime story of daring knights and terrifying dragons.

If Milcah's mother and father were worried about how they would feed the newest baby on the way, they did not mention it where Milcah could hear. Neither did they mention their concern over Milcah's mother's strange tiredness and breathlessness, which was far worse than it had been for any of her previous pregnancies.

But, Milcah's father reasoned to her mother, after all the little ones had gone to sleep, that they were both older now, and caring for children while carrying another was tiring work. It was only natural that Milcah's mother would find pregnancy a little harder at thirty than she had at twenty, and there was little to worry about when she was so experienced in the battle of childbirth now. First she had had

Milcah, and then three sets of twins—Rachel and Leah, Scott and Russell, and Dale and Grace—and all of them had been healthy with a fierce pair of lungs to herald their arrival in the world. Based on the size of Milcah's mother's bump, they would only be blessed with one child this time, and one baby would be easy after caring for so many pairs, especially now that Milcah was old enough to be of help.

"But *when* will the baby come?" Milcah asked her mother for the fifth evening in a row, when her mother had been pregnant seemingly forever.

"Soon, Milcah," her mother said with a smile, as she had the past several times. "Any day now."

"Tomorrow?" Milcah asked.

Her mother laughed. "I don't know, Milcah," she said. "The baby will arrive when he or she decides to arrive. They can't be rushed, and they don't follow anyone's schedule except their own."

"But it *might* be tomorrow?"

Her mother ruffled her hair. "Yes, Milcah," she said. "It might be tomorrow. It might be a week. It might be a while yet. You never quite know."

"I hope it's soon," Milcah said.

"So do I, little one," her mother replied. "I'm getting too large to walk."

Her father chuckled. "You'll have to take good care of your mama once the baby comes, Milcah. She'll be exhausted. She'll need you more than ever."

Milcah nodded seriously and curled up against her mother's side, resting her head atop her huge stomach. Her mother wrapped an arm around her, pulling her even closer.

"What about me?" her younger sister Rachel asked, scrambling across the room to join them.

"You as well," their father said. He picked up his seven-year-old daughter and swung her onto his lap. "The whole family will need all of you."

Rachel's twin sister Leah ran after her and clambered onto their father's lap too. The four younger siblings were all asleep in their corner of the room, but the three oldest were all allowed to stay up a little later, and no matter how tired Milcah might be, she could not bear to miss a single moment with her parents and sisters, not even to sleep.

"I hope it's a girl!" Leah said. "Girls are much more fun than boys."

"Whether they're a boy or a girl, I know you'll welcome them and love them just the same," their father said.

Leah nodded. "But a sister would be better please."

Their mother laughed. "All right, Leah," she said. "I'll see what I can do. But for now, I think it's bedtime for all of you. Your father and I as well, I think. It's been a long day."

"Tell us another story before we go to sleep!" Rachel said, wrapping her arms around her father's neck. "Please."

He chuckled. "I don't think your brothers and sister would like it if they found out I'd told you the next part of the story while they were sleeping, do you?"

"It doesn't have to be about Sir Boldheart," Milcah said quickly. "It could be another story."

Rachel gave her an annoyed look that suggested that 'another story' was not what she had had in mind, but her expression brightened again when her father went, "All right, all right. If it'll get you all to sleep with good dreams. Have I ever told you the story of Sir Boldheart's childhood friend, Lord Elroy?"

All three girls shook their heads.

"Well," their father began, "he was a cowardly boy, but one day, he wandered into the forest too deep…."

Milcah drifted to sleep in her mother's arms, listening to her father's soothing voice.

The next morning, Milcah's mother looked a little pale, but she smiled and hugged her daughter as Milcah scurried off to the mines. Never had she wanted to stay home with her mama more, but Milcah knew that if she did not go, there would be less food at the end of the day, and her mama and papa would almost certainly choose to go hungry themselves to give what food there was to the children.

Besides, Milcah knew that when the baby came, she and her sisters would be sent out of the house to stay with one of their neighbours. Last time, it had been old Mrs, Smith, a kindly widow whose grandchildren had all long since grown, and so who never missed an opportunity to fuss over the children or listen to their stories. Milcah thought she wouldn't mind sitting around Mrs. Smith's hearth with all her siblings, staying up far later into the night than they were ever usually allowed, waiting to find out whether the new baby was a boy or a girl and hearing stories of when Mrs. Smith. was young, when England was ruled by a prince, not a queen, and there were no steam engines to fuel with coal, so the mines did not even exist.

Milcah walked in the direction of the mines, her mind full of thoughts of new babies and of the strangeness of a world that existed long before she herself had been born. But the mine soon jolted her out of her daydreams. It was a terribly noisy place, with the thunder, or lift, that brought men up and down from far below the surface, and the rattle of the wheels of carts of coal. Pit ponies, half-blind from their existence in the darkness of the tunnels, neighed and snorted, and men shouted greetings and instructions to one another over the chaos.

Milcah had never been down into the mines themselves, but she still felt a little chill of fear every time she saw men step into the great iron lift and begin to descend. She could not fully imagine the horror of being trapped underground, with tons and tons of rock and earth separating you from the open sky, forced to dig deeper and hope that the walls would hold. The men would emerge from the mines with their faces blackened, blinking at the rush of sunlight, and Milcah always shivered to imagine how hard it must have been for them to breathe down there in the dark.

Milcah sometimes overheard her mama say that if anything went wrong while a man was down in the mines, only God could save him. "It doesn't matter a man's wits, or his skill, or how careful he might be. He can do little to save himself when the air is gone and the ceiling is falling in. And while we trust in the Lord," she said, with a sad shake of her head, "the masters should use the brains and pity He gave them to care for their men, instead of leaving them to hope for miracles."

Milcah did not think she was meant to hear these speeches. She was certain her mama would have spoken more quietly if she had known her daughter was awake. Occasionally, the topic of conversation arose when *something* happened in the mines—some event that the adults would not tell the children much about, but which shook the ground something fierce and meant that some workers would never return home again. More often, Milcah overheard this speech when her father tentatively raised the idea that *he* might find employment in the mines to better feed the family. After her mother's panicked lecture, he would not raise the idea for quite a while again.

But the area around the mines was safe enough, or so Milcah always thought. If it wasn't, her mama would never have allowed her to go there. You had to keep your wits about you, because there was so much *activity,* and the men had little time to worry about whether a little girl might be in their path as they transported their black treasure out of the mines.

By the end of the day, Milcah's skin would always be smeared with black, and her body would ache from all the walking back and forth and crouching to collect little fragments of coal from the ground. She could always feel the coal dust in the air, too, scraping her throat and making her cough, but she never complained, knowing she was lucky to be up here under the open sky and not down in the pits and tunnels below.

Some children were far less lucky. Young boys and girls were used to squeeze into spaces too small for any grown man, and Milcah knew of children who worked as door keepers, spending their days sitting in the dark on the edge of the tracks, waiting for the signal to open the doors to allow the carts to pass. Sometimes children fell asleep while alone in the dark, and then when the cart finally came....

Yes, Milcah thought. She was incredibly lucky.

It was midway through the afternoon when Milcah spotted her sister Leah racing across the mines toward her. Leah never came to the mines; she was too scared of the noise and the chaos, and instead always stayed home with mama to help with the mending and keep an eye on the younger ones. But Leah was running through the yard now, her braided hair flying out behind her, paying no mind to the racket and bustle around her.

"Milcah!" she shouted, loudly enough that several people looked up.

Milcah hurried towards her. "I'm here, Leah," she said. "What's wrong?"

Leah skidded to a stop in front of her, gasping for breath. "Something's wrong with mama," she said. "I can't find papa, and there's something wrong with mama."

Terror flooded Milcah. She did not pause to ask any more questions. She set off running in the direction of home, Leah scrambling to keep pace beside her.

"Is it the baby?" Milcah gasped, as they skidded out of the mines.

"I don't know!" Leah cried. "She was screaming, and I didn't know what to do, and she sent me out of the house—"

Rachel was sitting a little way beyond the front of their home with the younger twins in the dirt around her. She was hugging little three-year-old Grace, while Scott and Russell traced patterns in the earth.

"Mrs. Smith is here," Rachel said in a hushed voice as her sisters approached. "She said we should stay out here…."

"Mama's been crying," Grace mumbled, her face pressed against Rachel's shoulder.

"But she hasn't in a little while now," Rachel said, patting her youngest sister on the head. "Maybe she's feeling better."

"Did papa come home?" Milcah asked. Her sisters shook their heads.

Dread weighed down Milcah's stomach. "I'll go in," she said. "I'll see if she's all right."

But as Milcah walked up the front path, the door opened, and Mrs. Smith stepped out. Her hands and dress were stained with blood, and her pale face was stained with tears. She stared at the sky for a moment, not seeming to notice Milcah's presence at all, and wiped under her eyes with the back of her hand. She left blood smeared on her cheek.

"Mrs. Smith?" Milcah said.

Mrs. Smith jumped. Her wide eyes fell on Milcah. "Milcah," she said.

"What's wrong?" Milcah asked, but she felt almost certain that she did not want to know the answer. "Where's mama?"

Mrs. Smith looked at her with such pity that Milcah immediately wanted to take the question back, to never have asked it, to never have even *thought* it. But the words were out in the world now, and even before Mrs Smith spoke, Milcah knew what her answer would be.

“I’m so sorry, dear,” Mrs Smith said. “But she’s with the Lord now. She’s at peace.”

Milcah began to sob.

CHAPTER TWO

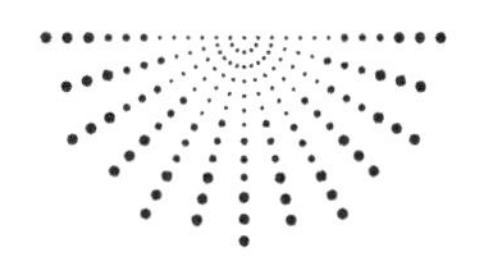

Milcah's new baby brother survived a day longer than their mother, and then he too succumbed to the trauma of his birth and left with the angels. At least, that was how Milcah's father described it, when he told the other children of his loss. Milcah had not seen any angels in the house, and besides, angels were supposed to be *good,* weren't they? Why would they carry her baby brother away when they could have let him live instead?

That night, Mrs. Smith came over to the house with a few scraps of food and made the family a stew to keep their strength up. It tasted of nothing in Milcah's mouth. She missed her mother so much it felt as though someone had driven a knife straight into her chest and ripped half of her heart away. The pain was a real, physical thing, in stark contrast to the numbness that spread through her arms and legs, and the hollowness in her head where her thoughts and her joy used to be.

Mrs. Smith helped the family when she could, but she was an elderly widow with barely enough resources for herself, and within days, Milcah's father was turning her help away, insisting with a false smile that they deeply appreciated her help but had every material thing they needed. But Mrs. Smith still insisted on looking after the littlest ones, while their father worked and Rachel and Leah joined Milcah in scouring the mines for scraps of coal.

A few days after their mother's death, Milcah returned home from the mines, her feet aching almost enough to distract her from the ache in her heart. She was covered in grime, and her stomach felt raw with hunger, but when she stumbled into the empty house ahead of her sisters, she felt her heart break all over again as she saw the unlit hearth and the absence of her mother's smiling face.

There was a gaping hole in their family, and although Milcah could never hope to fill it completely, she had to do whatever she could to help her father and her siblings now.

She had never cooked alone before, but her mother had allowed her to help occasionally, so she knew at least some of the basics. And *somebody* needed to do it. They could not rely on Mrs. Smith forever, and her father was always exhausted after working so hard since dawn in the fields. If nothing else, at least the sight of a hot dinner on the stove when he returned might make him smile.

The larder was almost bare, but Milcah's mother had always been able to produce delicious meals from the sparsest and simplest of ingredients, so Milcah refused to be deterred. She could prepare a stew, at least, to fill everyone's bellies and warm them up after a long, hard day.

The cooking turned out to be more difficult than Milcah expected, and she was often blinded by her tears as she felt the gaping absence of her mother beside her. But Milcah was undeterred, and by the time their father walked through the door, a thick vegetable stew was bubbling atop the stove.

He walked across the room to her, moving more slowly than he had before, and looked at the meal, before pressing a kiss to the crown of his daughter's head.

"Thank you," he murmured into her hair, and Milcah felt herself smiling for the first time in days.

Milcah was disappointed with the stew when it was finally finished. It didn't taste like the ones her mother had made at all, and she looked sadly up at her father, certain he would be disappointed too. But he ate the meal quickly, and after he was done, he smiled at Milcah again and told her it had been delicious. When all her siblings agreed, Milcah felt a warmth in her heart that made all her effort worthwhile.

She would try again and do even better tomorrow.

Over the next several months, life continued much the same. Milcah turned ten, an age that she felt should confer all the wisdom and responsibility required for her to step into her mother's place and support her family, and which therefore made her deeply sad to realise that she had undergone no magical transformation, and that the gap left by her mother was exactly as it had been before.

She continued to cook, and gradually developed a knack for the art, despite her tender age and the lack of abundant ingredients. Her favourite part of every day was watching her father take his first bite of whatever she had created, and seeing the smile spread slowly across his face. Once, he told her that her cooking made him feel as though her mother was still with them, and the words made Milcah's heart sing, even as they reminded her of all they had lost.

One day, Milcah's father was late returning from tilling the neighbour's land, and Milcah was beginning to worry when she heard the familiar rattle of her father's cart outside. She hurried out and then stopped short in the doorway when she saw a large arm hanging over the side of the cart.

"Papa?" she asked, running forward. "Is that—"

"He's not dead," her papa said. "Thank the Lord. I found him in the river. He was drifting downstream. He jumped into the back of the cart and hauled the man up.

Milcah was no judge of grown-up's ages, but he looked about the same age as her father, with a slightly scruffy brown beard and surprisingly bushy eyebrows. His skin was pale, as though he wasn't much used to the sun, and his clothes were bedraggled from the river.

Her father groaned from the effort as he hauled the man over his shoulder and began to carry him towards the house.

"Who is he?" Milcah asked, running along beside him.

"I don't know," her father said. "I've not seen him around town."

"What are you going to do with him?"

"Take care of him, Milcah. Give him dinner once he wakes up, and see how else we can help."

Milcah stopped. "We can't do that, papa," she said. "We barely even have enough food for ourselves."

"That is all the more reason to have empathy for those who are even less fortunate than ourselves," her father said patiently. "We must always help people in need, just as we would hope others would help us if we found ourselves in such a situation."

Milcah considered his words as he carried the man into the house. Perhaps it was like Mrs. Smith helping them after her mother had died, she thought. Mrs. Smith had little of her own, but she was still determined to share it with them. And just as they had appreciated her kindness and support, they needed to offer that kindness to others, regardless of their own meagre means.

Her father laid the man down in his own bed and asked Milcah to bring him some water. The man mumbled slightly as her father helped him to sit up and poured a little water past his lips, but he did not awaken.

Her younger brothers and sisters asked a hundred questions about the man, but their father had no answers to give them. None of them recognised him, and their father could not guess how he had ended up unconscious and feverish in the river. Perhaps he had slipped and fallen upstream, he said, or had been the victim of some brutal attempt to end his life. In the end, he told them, it did not truly matter. He was a man in need, and they had a duty to help him.

Their father slept on the floor that night, and Milcah lay awake for several hours, listening to the stranger's fevered mumblings. She wondered who he was, and if he had a family. How would they feel once they realised he was missing? If he did not recover, they might never learn what had become of him. How would she feel if her father simply never returned home one day? She would not be able to bear it.

She needed to do what she could to help this man.

The following morning, her father left to work the fields, and Milcah remained behind to care for the stranger and keep an eye on her youngest siblings. She prepared a light broth to try and sustain the man, and with her younger brothers' help, she was able to prop the man up enough to press a few spoonfuls to his mouth.

Midway through the afternoon, the stranger stirred. He gave out a deep groan, and then he blinked several times, taking in the unfamiliar room.

“Where am I?” he mumbled. His voice was hoarse.

“You’re in Norton,” Milcah said. “My papa said he found you in the river. You were nearly dead, he said. But you’re all right, I think.”

“Your papa?” the man asked. He pressed a hand to his forehead and groaned again.

“His name is Murray Fox,” Milcah said. “I don’t—I don’t think you know him, sir. He said you were a stranger.”

“Then why did he help me?” The man blinked again and then looked around, taking in the sparsely furnished room.

“Because you needed help, sir,” Milcah said. She turned to Russell, one of her six-year-old brothers. “Russell, run to the neighbours and see if you can find papa. Tell him the man is awake.”

Russell nodded and scampered off, and Milcah turned back to the man.

“Are you hungry, sir?”

He shook his head slowly. “You don’t have to call me sir. I don’t deserve it,” he added, so quietly that Milcah thought perhaps she was not meant to hear it.

“Then what’s your name?” Milcah asked.

“Gerry,” he said.

She tried to give him an encouraging smile. “I’m Milcah,” she said.

Gerry was a quiet guest. He spoke little after giving his name, and he spent more time looking at the wall beside the bed than at Milcah or anything else in the room. When

Milcah's father returned, he spoke to Gerry in a kindly voice, and the two of them exchanged a few words that were too low for Milcah to hear.

Milcah set about preparing the evening meal as the stranger drifted off to sleep again. They had very little food in their stores—even less, now they had fed the stranger and lost work hours to caring for him—but she was certain she could muster up something. The stranger needed his strength.

He woke up in time to eat the stew that Milcah prepared him, and he smiled and thanked her quietly, complimenting her on the quality of her cooking. He drifted off again before the rest of the family had time to eat the scraps that were left. Milcah's father passed out soon after him, but the children were too full of excitement and hunger to settle.

"Milcah, I'm *hungry*," little Russell whined, pulling on her sleeve. "I want more food."

"Hush," Milcah said quietly. "There is no more food tonight."

"But I'm *hungry*," Russell said again.

"Well, there'll be more food tomorrow."

"That man got more to eat," Russell's twin brother Scott said, pointing at the sleeping stranger. "Why does he get some and we don't?"

"Because he's sick," Milcah said. "He needs it more than we do."

"But it's *our* food."

Milcah glanced over at the stranger. He was still sleeping, his back turned to them. "Hush, now," she said. "He might hear you. He's our guest, Scott. We should always be kind to others, and help them however we can. God brought this man into our lives for a reason. We are meant to help him. The fact that we don't know him doesn't matter. Remember what we learned at church? Sometimes we might even host angels unawares."

Her younger siblings fell silent, considering her words.

But little did she suspect that their guest was very much awake on his bed, and listening to every word she spoke. When he heard Milcah refer to *angels,* tears ran down his cheeks. He was as far from being an angel as dark was from light. This family had given him their last morsels of food, when he did not deserve a crumb discarded by even the richest man. If they truly knew who he was….

But perhaps, he thought, with some bewilderment, that would not matter to them. He only deserved their resentment, but their generosity and their simple honest faith made him wonder if they would still help him, even if they knew the truth.

The thought only made him feel even more guilty.

But Milcah knew none of this. She got her siblings ready for bed, and shushed them again as they began speculating about who the stranger might really be.

"Maybe he's a spy!" Leah murmured excitedly, and Milcah had to glare at her for joining the littler ones in their nonsense.

"Hush," she said again. "He might hear. It doesn't matter who he is."

But Milcah had to admit that she was curious too.

When they woke up the following morning, the stranger was gone.

"Maybe he *was* an angel!" Russell exclaimed, but Milcah saw the concerned look on her father's face, and she did not believe it.

"I hope he is all right, papa," she said softly.

Her father still looked worried, but he nodded. "We helped him, and that is what matters. He was clearly strong enough to move on, and we must respect that."

But Milcah still burned with curiosity. They had never even learned the stranger's full name.

CHAPTER THREE

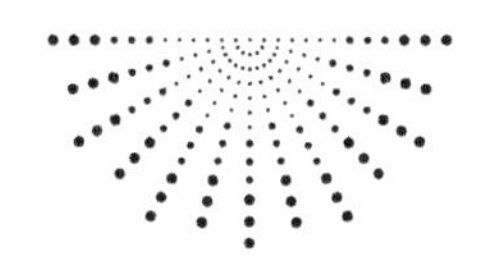

As time passed, the family forgot the stranger known only as Gerry and the mystery surrounding him. They had too many cares and concerns about the here and now to reflect much on what was now far out of their ability to help.

Milcah's father's land gave poorer and poorer returns with each passing year, and some of his neighbours, perhaps sensing his desperation, began offering less pay for more work. Milcah's father, a widower with seven children to feed and no other family to speak of or turn to for help, could do little to protest.

In order to keep themselves fed, all of the children began collecting coal from around the mines. Even the youngest ones, little Grace and Dale, barely five years old, were soon spending their days covered with grime, collecting fragments of that black gold to fund their own suppers.

It worried Milcah more than she could put into words. The younger ones had constant coughs, and she was convinced it was from breathing in all the dust from the mines while they were still so small and delicate. They were sickly, too, always tired, and although Milcah tried her hardest to cook them hearty meals to keep up their strength, she could not perform miracles, and the ingredients that they could afford often left their bellies hungry.

Milcah worried for her father too. He was not particularly old, she knew, for a grown up at least, but he did such intense physical work for long hours every day, and he often refused to eat himself if it meant the children would have more to eat. She did not know how much longer he would be able to maintain it.

The mines were also not safe to work around, even without the dust. Cave-ins and ceiling collapses were common, and although they did not usually affect those above the ground, there was no guarantee. A mine collapse beneath your feet could kill you just as surely as one above your head.

Her brothers Scott and Russell began to pester their father about their desire to work in the mines properly, to earn better money for the family, but their father refused them point blank. He had seen too many families torn apart by the terrible conditions in the mines, too many men left crippled and unable to work by horrific accidents, too many children killed by accidents simply because they were too small for the workers to see.

Milcah wished she could forbid her sisters from working above ground around the mines as well. When they had all been smaller, they had mostly been ignored by the men who worked there, but now they were a little more grown, they had begun to attract unsettling attention. Milcah was tall for a fourteen-year-old, if a little reedy from being underfed, with a quiet confidence that many men seemed eager to punish her for. She hated the comments and the whistles she got from the men as she worked, but she was more concerned for Leah and Rachel. At twelve, they should both have been too young to attract that sort of attention in the first place, but their age did not seem to stop the men around them.

Whenever Rachel got a comment, she glared at whoever had spoken to her, while Leah would blush and shrink away. Milcah was not certain which reaction was worse. Appearing too weak might encourage the men to push on, enjoying the discomfort they were causing, but appearing too strong might anger the men. All Milcah could do was pray that the comments never escalated into anything worse.

"I wish we could live elsewhere, papa," she said to her father quietly one night, when all the others were asleep. "I know Sheffield is our home, but—"

"I know," her father said. He sounded exhausted. "I know, Milcah. I wish we could too."

"Then why don't we?"

Her father sighed. "This is our home, Milcah. I grew up here. I married your mother here. This is the last place we saw her. I hate to think that it will have driven us away."

Milcah did not press the matter. She understood her father's reluctance. This house was the only home she had ever known, and the land and the village around it were full of memories of her mother. But she worried that if they did not leave this place, it would eventually kill at least one more of them.

Yet pressuring her father would not change things. The idea was in both of their minds, and now she had to give him time to consider it.

But less than a week later, events came to a head. It was a grey, dreary autumn afternoon, and Milcah was collecting coal when she heard Rachel shouting. She looked up to see a man with his hand on Leah's arm, leering at her while she shrunk away, and Rachel running toward them.

"Oi!" Rachel shouted. "Get your grubby hand off her."

"Why?" the man said. His grip on Leah's arm tightened, and Leah winced. "Feeling left out, are ya?"

Milcah hurried toward them too, but she knew she couldn't reach him before Rachel did.

"Leave my sister alone!" Rachel said. "She wants nothing to do with you."

Leah shook her head at her sister, looking panicked, but Rachel did not slow down. "I said," she repeated, as she reached them, *"leave her alone."* She grabbed the man's hand and tried to pull it away from her sister.

The man responded by grabbing Rachel's arm and hauling her closer to him, almost pulling her off her feet. "Don't get involved in things you don't understand, little missy," he hissed.

Rachel responded by spitting in his face.

The man let out a howl of rage as the spit hit him in the eye. He released Leah, but his grip on Rachel tightened.

"You little brat," he said. "You want my attention? Well, now you've got it. And you're such a pretty little thing."

"Sir!" Milcah shouted, her heart racing so hard she felt almost sick. "Please forgive her. She's just a child."

The man looked Rachel up and down, leering. "Don't look like much of a child to me," he said.

"Please, sir," Milcah said. It made her skin crawl to address such a man with any sort of respect, but she had to convince him to calm down, before her sisters got seriously hurt. The man had strong muscles and a hard face from working in the mines, and even if the three of them all fought him with all of their might, Milcah did not believe they could escape him if he did not want to let them go.

"Give me one reason why I should?" the man said. "Seems to me like the girl could do with a good lesson in respect."

"Please," Milcah said again. "She's rash, but she's only twelve."

The man gave Milcah a closer look, and his grin grew. "How about you then, girlie? What are you offering if I let her go, eh?"

Milcah felt her face burning, but she refused to look away from him. "Please," she said again.

The man snorted. He released Rachel's arm, revealing bright bruises where his fingers had dug into her skin. He took a purposeful step towards Milcah, and Milcah struggled not to flinch. Behind him, she saw Rachel standing tall again, steeling herself to fight back, and she gave her younger sister a warning with her eyes. Rachel looked about to argue, when a loud voice called across the yard.

"Fenton!" the man said. "Fenton, what do you think you're doing? You better get back to work right this minute, or the boss'll have your head!"

The man paused, scowling. "In a minute, Thomas!" he shouted.

But Thomas shook his head. "It's gotta be now, Fenton."

The man named Fenton reached forward and seized Milcah's wrist, squeezing so hard she thought he might be trying to break it. "This isn't over, missy," he said. "When I see you and your sisters again... well. We're going to have a conversation, you and I."

He released Milcah's wrist and strode away.

"What on earth do you think you're playing at?" Milcah hissed at Rachel, after the man had gone. "He could have hurt you!"

"He was going to hurt Leah!" Rachel said. She wrapped an arm around her twin sister and glowered at Milcah, as though she were somehow at fault.

"You only made the situation worse," Milcah said.

"I was defending my sister. Was I supposed to just do nothing? Or be *polite* to him, like you were?"

Milcah did not know what to say. Her sister was right, in her own way. She certainly could not leave her sister to face such a threatening man alone, and she had loathed being polite to the brute. But sometimes there was no better choice, and she told her sister as much.

"It isn't safe here, Rachel," she said. "Not for any of us. We have to be careful."

"We shouldn't have to be careful!" Rachel said. "It's men like him who should be careful. They should be the ones who have to watch what they say."

"I know, Rachel," Milcah said softly. "I know." She felt as though she were about to cry, and she blinked furiously to keep the tears away. "The world isn't as it should be. But as long as we're here—"

"I don't want to be here," Leah murmured. "It's frightening, Milcah."

"Don't worry, Leah," Rachel said. "You'll always have me here to protect you."

But Leah shook her head. "Not always," she said. "And what will happen then?"

Tears ran down her face, and Milcah's heart broke to see her.

"Leah?" she said softly, dreading the answer. "Has something worse happened?"

Leah shook her head. "No," she whispered. "But I'm scared it will."

Milcah took in her sister's terrified face, and she reached a decision. "All right," she said. "We're going home now. All of us. We need to talk to papa about this."

Milcah was worried what their papa would say, but any fears turned out to be unnecessary. Their father took one look at the bruises forming on all three of the girls' arms, and his face turned red with anger. When he asked who did this to them, Milcah refused to give a name, telling their father that it might have been anyone. She told him how many men had been making comments or leering at the sisters in full view of everyone else in the mines, and how much she feared for their safety, and slowly her father's face turned from a furious red to a terrified grey.

"It isn't safe, papa," Milcah finished softly, and her father shook his head.

"No, Milcah," he said. "You're right. It's not."

The very next day, he started preparing for them to move away.

CHAPTER FOUR

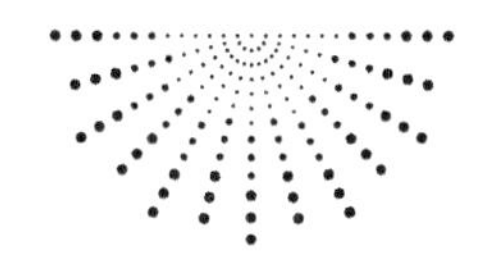

They did not sell the farm. The land was so unprofitable that it would not have brought in much money, and although Milcah's father saw the need to move, he could not quite give up on his family home entirely just yet.

Milcah's father thought he knew of some relatives of their mother in South Devon, and so, it was decided, that would be where they would go. Milcah had never even heard of a place called South Devon, and when she asked her father if it was farther away than

Manchester, he only smiled sadly and told her it was far farther than that.

“Farther than London, even,” he said. “We're going right to the south of the country.”

Rachel screwed up her nose. “But we’re *Northerners,*” she said.

Their father chuckled. “Your mother wasn’t always. Her parents came from down south. I’m sure we’ll settle in just fine. And there’s no mines down there, you know. No dust. It’ll be a better life for us.”

Milcah did not ask what they would do for money without the mine nearby. Her entire family had kept themselves alive for years through hard work and a willingness to do whatever needed to be done. That experience would serve them well, wherever they ended up.

On the day of departure, their father sent the little ones around the house twice over, looking for anything they might have forgotten. They could not bring most of the furniture with them, but the family had few possessions enough that they would all fit in their father's cart, along with the siblings, as long as they were willing to squeeze. All of them insisted that a little discomfort would be nothing compared to leaving their treasures behind, but Milcah wondered whether they would still agree with that sentiment after a week on the road.

Milcah, as the oldest, would sit up front with her papa, helping him to drive. The mule they owned was not particularly fast, but he was a hardy thing, named Sir Boldheart by Dale after the knight in their father's childhood stories. They would not move anywhere near as quickly as rich people, with their grand carriages and constant changing of horses, but they would move steadily enough, and that was what mattered.

As their papa called that it was time to leave, Milcah looked around the empty house, making sure every little detail of it was safe in her memory. She remembered cosy evenings spent curled up on her mother's lap by the hearth, and games of chase played in the middle of the kitchen when she and Rachel and Leah were the only children in the house. For so many years, it had been the place where she felt safe in the world, the place where she truly belonged. The safety had been disrupted when her mother died, but it had still been *home,* still represented her family, right until the end. She would miss it.

"Milcah!" her father shouted again from outside. "We need to go!"

Milcah took one last look around the house and smiled, saying her silent goodbye.

The journey to South Devon was as long as it was uncomfortable. The cart was designed for transporting goods, not people, and its rickety wheels left all of them feeling dizzy and sore after a day's travel. It had no roof, either, so there was no protection for any of them from the rain, and as it was autumn in England, rain was an almost constant concern.

The family did not have much money to pay for rooms in inns, so they tended to stay in places that were willing to give them space—in a small room or maybe just in the barn—in exchange for work. Milcah ached from all the work and travel, but she appreciated the fresh, dust-less air all around them, and she tried to keep herself awake as they travelled, talking to her father and taking in the ever-changing scenery of the countryside around them. She had never seen any of England outside of their home village, and she was not going to miss this opportunity now.

When her younger siblings got restless, she distracted them with games, where they invented stories or looked for interesting things in the world around their rattling cart. She began to retell the tales of Sir Boldheart that she remembered from their father when they were younger, and they all giggled when they imagined Sir Boldheart not as the noble knight he always was, but as their own mule, dressed in finery and facing down dragons.

Their father had told fewer and fewer stories since their mother died, always exhausted by work and by heartbreak, but as the journey continued, he began to speak more and more, weaving new tales of Sir Boldheart and holding every one of his children rapt on his every word.

Despite the discomfort, and the rain, and the homesickness, Milcah realised that she was happy. They slowly trundled their way across the country, listening to and inventing stories, hearing their father share knowledge about different birds and animals they saw that Milcah had never known he possessed, and despite the lack of walls, despite the lack of a home, Milcah felt safe for the first time in a good long while. Within a couple of weeks, even the younger ones' coughs seemed to heal, and the usually shy Leah spoke more and laughed louder as the mines faded into a memory, long behind them.

Still, they were all excited and relieved when they arose one morning and overheard the innkeeper telling their father that their destination was only about five miles away. Their mother's relatives came from a place called Beer, right on the coast, and although Rachel giggled at the name slightly, their father insisted that their mother's tales of the place had made it sound like paradise. He had not yet been able to contact any family members, but he had written ahead, he told them, to arrange a place for them to live.

Milcah had never been near the sea before, but she imagined she could smell it on the air as they approached that day. The air felt fresher than even the pure country air they'd been travelling through for the past few weeks, and it had a slight saltiness to it that made Milcah want to take deep breaths of it, and have all her tiredness melt away.

"Look!" Scott said from the back of the cart, after another couple of hours' travel. "Look over there!"

Milcah looked where he was pointing, and she gasped. There, on the horizon, she could see the white-capped blue of the sea.

All the siblings squabbled with one another as they tried to stand up and get the best view, and even Milcah found herself craning her neck, trying to catch a better glimpse, while her father shouted at the others to settle down. But soon, they turned another corner, and the entire village came into view. It was a beautiful place, nestled on white cliffs above the bay. The sea lapped gently against the beach, where several fishing boats had been pulled up onto shore. She could see several more out in the water, performing their day's work.

A couple of small figures seemed to be walking the cliffs, looking out across the sea, and Milcah's heart leapt to see them. Soon, she thought, *she* could walk there too.

The village itself looked even smaller than their home village of Norton, built almost entirely of white brick buildings with dark roofs. Milcah took her father's hand as she looked at their new home, and he smiled at her and squeezed it gently.

"Not bad, eh?" he asked her.

"No," she murmured. "Not bad at all."

CHAPTER FIVE

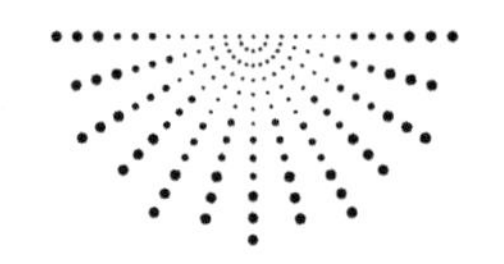

Their new cottage looked right out over the water, with just a small sloping scramble down to sea itself. The building itself was in rough shape, with cobwebs up the chimney and holes in the roof, but Milcah's family was used to difficult conditions and hard work, and the surroundings and low price more than made up for the problems they found. The sea breeze was bracing, but it still felt warmer down in Beer than it had in Sheffield, and even cloudy days had a certain romanticism to them when looking out across the bay.

Things were not perfect. They soon realised that any remaining relatives had either moved away or died several years before, so they had no connections to help them. Still, Beer was a small village, where newcomers were soon noticed and discussed, and the Fox family were soon known to everybody as relatives of Old Joe and his daughter. If people in the small village were generally wary of outsiders, they were welcoming to those who they believed truly "belonged" to Beer, even before they arrived, and Milcah and her family soon felt at home.

Milcah's father found a job as a fisherman, while Milcah and her sisters took work at a fishmongers in the nearby town of Seaton, just a mile's walk away. The fish smelt awful, but at least the smell could not hurt them, the way the coal dust could, and Milcah found she did not mind the stench, as long as her family were all safe and well-fed. Her younger siblings were much quicker to complain, but they loved running along the beach, picking up shingles and tossing them into the water, hearing the caw of seagulls and watching the fishermen out at sea.

There was much more food now too, and always plenty of fish for all of them to eat, and Milcah loved experimenting with new recipes. The first time she brought fish home to cook, nine-year-old Dale screwed up his nose and flinched away, declaring that he would *never* eat anything so disgusting, but he changed his tune as soon as he smelled the delicious aroma from Milcah's frying pan, and the whole family laughed when he not only ate his entire serving but eagerly begged his sister for seconds too.

Milcah loved the chance to work for her family without risking her own safety. She loved trusting that her younger siblings had fresh air to breathe, and that her father was being compensated for the work that he did. Most of all, she loved the time she got to herself now, walking quietly along the cliffs and the beach, breathing in the smell of the ocean and feeling truly at peace. The younger ones were even getting a little bit of schooling, and Milcah began to teach herself her letters too, when she had the chance. She was glad that her mother moved away from the village, as otherwise she never would have met Milcah's father at all, but Milcah did wonder what appeal Sheffield could have held for her, when her home was like this.

Of course, Milcah missed Sheffield herself, more often than she had expected. She missed the face of Mrs. Layton at the grocery store, and the rolling hills around their village, and the familiar paths and fields she had walked ever since she first learned how. But that, Milcah thought, was because Norton was her first home. If Beer had been her mother's first home, she did not see why she would have left.

Scott and Russell were particularly thrilled by their new home. Although they all loved their father's tales of Sir Boldheart, the boys were of an age now where they delighted in more dastardly stories, and the legends of the smugglers' caves around Beer provided the perfect source for them. They were full of stories about the legendary fisherman and smuggler Jack Rattenbury, more than half of which Milcah was certain they had made up themselves, and their father frequently had to punish them for trying to explore the caves that were still sometimes used to store smuggled goods to that day. They were so obsessed that young Dale started declaring his intention to become a smuggler too when he grew up, causing their father to give him a stern lecture about morals and responsibility while barely being able to hide his amusement at his youngest son's imagination.

Two years passed in Beer in relative comfort. The family gained strength from the fish and the fresh sea air, and they worked tirelessly to fix the holes in the roof of their rented cottage and even save up a little coin in case they ever found themselves in dangerous circumstances again.

But their newfound peace could not last. Milcah, Leah and Rachel walked home from the fishmongers in Seaton, with Rachel chattering about the handsome new apprentice the family had taken on, and Leah complaining that they *really* needed to get work selling fish in Beer instead, because the mile's walk was far too much after a long day at work. Milcah smiled at her sisters, enjoying, as she did every evening, the view of the sea.

When they reached home, their father had not yet returned, but that was not incredibly unusual, so they all set about preparing dinner with the fish they had brought back from Seaton. Milcah had taught both her sisters something about cooking in the intervening years, but they tended to do the work methodically and a little begrudgingly, treating it as a chore and not as a joy. Milcah, on the other hand, still loved to create new recipes, and considered her time in the kitchen to be the part of the day that all of the rest of it was leading toward.

When dinner was ready and their father had not yet returned, Milcah insisted that the others eat, while she lingered by the window, hoping for a glimpse of her father walking home. She saw no sign of him.

Another hour passed, and Milcah began to worry. Her father was never so late home, and Milcah began to imagine that something terrible had happened. Life in Beer was generally safe, and the weather had not been too rough out to sea that day, but accidents could still happen.

Forcing herself to appear calm to her younger siblings, she declared that she was walking down to the beach to look for their father and hurry him home. Leah shot her a worried look, but the younger ones seemed mostly unconcerned.

Milcah pulled on her cloak and stepped out into the twilight air. The night was a little chilly, and she walked briskly towards the beach.

Even from a distance, she could see that the boat her father usually used was already pulled up onto the shore. She ran the rest of the way, sliding on the stony beach as she went, and stopped directly in front of her father's boat, gasping for breath.

The shore was quiet, with not a soul in sight. But as Milcah looked, she spotted dried blood in the bottom of her father's boat, and more patches of it forming a faint trail across the stones.

Her heart in her throat, Milcah ran up the beach toward a nearby pub. A fisherman that she knew worked with her father was standing outside, his hands in his pockets, and he winced when he saw Milcah approaching.

"You're Murray Fox's oldest lass," he said. It didn't sound like a question, but Milcah nodded anyway.

"What's happened?" she asked.

"Now remember, lass," he said. "Your father's alive, and that's the most important thing, now."

Milcah felt herself go white. People only commented on someone being alive if they very nearly were not.

"Where is he?" she gasped. Her voice cracked.

"Inside, lass," he said. "But perhaps you shouldn't—"

Milcah strode past him without waiting for him to finish. Whatever had happened, she needed to see it for herself. Nothing would be worse than the fears now filling her imagination.

She pushed open the front door of the pub and marched inside. Then she froze in the doorway as she took in the scene that awaited her.

Her father lay atop a large table in the centre of the pub, while several men and the landlord's wife all crowded around him. Milcah still could not see him clearly, but she could see the blood that stained his clothes, and the cloths wrapped around his leg and his face, and she could hear his quiet moans, even from the doorway.

"Papa?" She pushed her way through the crowd. "What happened?"

He looked worse up close than he had from a distance. His right leg was being supported by a wooden splint, but it still looked *wrong* somehow, positioned in an unnatural way. His hands were bandaged too, and the landlord's wife was currently fashioning a sling for his oddly bent arm. He appeared to be unconscious, and that was fortunate, Milcah thought, because he was moaning in pain, and through the bandages she could see a large, bloody gash in his face, running from his mouth almost to his eye.

"What happened?" she said again, looking at the men around him.

"There was an accident, miss," one of the fishermen said. He said nothing more, and Milcah huffed with frustration.

"What kind of accident?"

"I fell overboard," one of the men said. He looked young, not much older than Milcah herself, and his face was stained with tear tracks. "I'm sorry, miss. Truly, I am. I should have been looking where I was going, and one of the other men knocked into me, and I tripped over the side of the boat."

Milcah stared at him. What did this have to do with her father's injuries?

"Well, good old Murray jumped right after him, didn't he?" another of the fishermen said. "Right into the water. Man's the weakest swimmer of all of us, not having lived here as a kid, but he didn't even hesitate."

"He grabbed me," the younger man said. "Hauled me to the side of the boat, insisted I climb in first. But then—" He cut himself off, unable to look at Milcah.

"He got caught by the tide," the second man said. "It's powerful fierce in that part of the bay. Jackson here was lucky he got back in the boat before it caught him. It threw your pa against the side of the boat, and then ripped him away before we could grab him."

Milcah desperately wanted to take her father's hand, to reassure him and to reassure herself, but she did not want to risk hurting him further. "Then what happened?" she whispered.

"He got dragged to the rocks," the older man said quietly. "They're sharp there, a bunch of them hiding beneath the surface. We thought he was dead for certain, and if anyone went in after him, they'd be dead too. But Johnson here refused to give up. Your da was near unconscious by this point, but we managed to throw a rope to him, and by the blessing of the Lord, he grabbed hold of it long enough for us to pull him away from the rocks so we could row closer and pull him aboard. But it was a nasty business, miss."

Milcah shook her head, tears burning in her eyes. Of course her father had become injured trying to save someone else from harm. It sounded just like him.

"Papa," she whispered.

"He'll live," another man said. He looked finer dressed than the others, and Milcah vaguely recognised him as the doctor from Seaton. He shopped in the fishmongers occasionally. He gave Milcah a sympathetic smile. "He'll need a lot of care for a while."

"But he'll get better?" Milcah asked.

He was silent for too long. Milcah knew his answer before he spoke it. "It will be difficult," he said eventually, which seemed like a long and gentle way of saying *no*. "His leg is broken in several places. He may not ever regain control of it fully. And he swallowed a lot of water, and took some damage to the face. There may be internal injuries that we cannot see."

Milcah swallowed, fighting back her tears. "When will we know?" she asked, if there's any —internal damage, as you say?"

"It will take time," the doctor said gently, "to understand all the long-term effects."

Milcah sniffed. “I should bring him home,” she said, but the doctor shook his head.

“We cannot disturb him tonight,” he said. “We need to give his body a little more time to recover before we move it again. The landlord here has kindly allowed him to remain.”

Milcah turned to the landlord. “We have a little money,” she said. “Not much, but we can pay you for the bother—”

“No worrying about that, miss,” the landlord said. “Your pa’s a good man. One night won’t do much harm, now, will it?”

“Thank you,” Milcah whispered. She reached out and gently touched her father’s undamaged arm. “It’s all right, papa,” she said. “We’re all going to take care of you.”

CHAPTER SIX

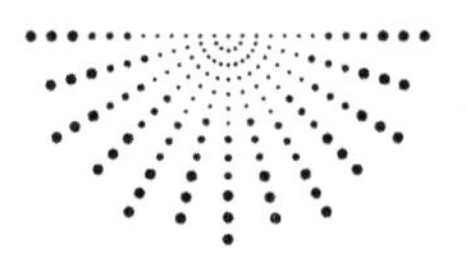

The Fox siblings helped to carry their father back home the following day. Milcah did what she could to prepare her brothers and sisters for the reality of their father's injuries, but words could not much soften their shock when they saw him with their own eyes.

Their father was conscious, at least, which the doctor assured Milcah was a good sign. Milcah was not so certain that he would not have been better asleep, as he groaned in pain with almost every step as his children and his fellow fishermen carried him back to his cottage.

Milcah reassured her youngest siblings that injuries sometimes happened, and that just as they sometimes fell and cut their knees and saw the scrapes heal with time, so too would their father return to his old self as long as he was given the chance to rest. But Milcah exchanged worried glances with Rachel and Leah when the others could not see. Some wounds, she knew, could not be healed.

Time passed, but their father did not recover. His arm and his broken leg both set wrong, making it difficult for him to walk and impossible for him to work. Their father's employer refused to offer any help or support, arguing that Murray *chose* to jump into the water, and that any inability to work was therefore his own fault. When Milcah attempted to convince him otherwise, he threatened to sue Murray for damage of company property—Murray's own body—and Milcah was forced to retreat.

The fellow fishermen on the boat that day gave them a little money and extra fish, as thanks for Murray's selflessness and bravery, but they did not have much of their own, and even less that they could spare. Milcah appreciated every morsel they received, knowing it was imbued with gratitude and kindness, but it was not enough to sustain them.

Milcah worked harder than ever, taking any hours at the fishmongers that were offered to her, and supplementing their income however she could in the evenings with any mending or laundry she could convince their neighbours to commission her for. It was an exhausting existence, but with her siblings also doing whatever work they could, they managed to continue to pay the rent on the cottage and all remained fed, and Milcah scraped and saved every spare penny, determined to have as much money as she possibly could in reserve in case another disaster ever befell them.

For her father's physical injuries were not the most concerning reminder of his accident. Murray Fox had always been a strong and healthy man before that day, even living, as he had, in the polluted air around the mines. But ever since the accident, he had difficulty breathing, and on his bad days, even walking across their small cottage was enough to exhaust him and leave him gasping. Worse, in Milcah's eyes, was the confusion. Her father had always been sharp of mind, but now he often seemed to lose the thread of the conversation, and would look at his own children with uncertainty for a few moments before recognition would spark again.

He still had good days, when he would sit in the fresh air outside the cottage, looking out at the sea, and then gather with his children in the evening and tell them stories of brave knights and daring smugglers and anything else he could conjure from his imagination. Milcah savoured every one of those days. Other times, he remained in bed, his broken bones aching, his mind unable to focus on any one thought for long.

"I wish there was something we could do for papa," her youngest sister Grace said one winter day, as their father moaned in pain beneath a pile of blankets, his bed dragged close to the fire.

Milcah wrapped an arm around her sister's shoulders. "You are already helping," she said. "You take care of him when he's feeling unwell, and you spend time with him when he is stronger. I know he treasures every minute he gets to spend with you. The best thing you can do is treasure your time with him in return."

Grace seemed comforted by Milcah's words, but when Milcah thought them over again later that night, they felt empty to her. What her father really needed was a way to get better, a return to his old strength and sharpness. But she knew that such a thing was impossible now, so instead she would do all she could to bring joy and security to him and to the rest of her beloved family.

One day, when Milcah was eighteen, she was sitting up late, doing some mending by the light of the dying fire, when she heard her father call out her name from his small bedroom. He had had a fairly good day, chatting and joking with the little ones and smiling as he gazed out to sea, but the pain in his limbs had sent him to bed early, and Milcah had thought him long since asleep.

She set down her mending and slowly entered the bedroom. “Yes, papa?” she asked quietly. “Is anything the matter?”

Her father shook his head. He was grimacing in pain, but his eyes were sharp, and he looked at Milcah with gentle determination. “No, love,” he said. “But I need to talk to you, while I’m thinking clearly.”

Milcah nodded and sat down carefully on the edge of her father’s bed. “What do you need, papa?”

"I am going to die, Milcah," he said hoarsely. "And sooner rather than later."

"Don't talk like that, papa," Milcah said. She clutched his hand, and he shook his head again.

"It's the way of the world, Milcah," he said. "The way the Lord intended it. We all pass from this world eventually. And although I am savouring all I can of this life while I am still in it, we both know that I will not struggle on like this forever. I am weak, Milcah. So I needed to speak with you now." He squeezed her hand. "When I pass, my dear, I want to be buried beside your mother, near our land in Sheffield."

"But papa—"

"I know it is far," her father said. "And I know this place has done so much good for all of us."

"It has not done us good," Milcah said. "It took your strength away from you."

"I gave it away," her father said, with a rueful smile. "I chose to risk it, to save another who needed it. I know this place has brought us all peace in its own way. But I am homesick, Milcah. I want to see the lands I grew up in again before I die, and if I cannot, then I at least wish to rest in them, with your mother by my side."

Milcah nodded, fighting back the tears that threatened to roll down her face. "Then that is what we shall do," she said. "Of course, that is what we shall do." She squeezed his hand tighter still. "I have some money saved," she said. "In case the family ever needed it. We can use it to get home."

Her father nodded, a small smile on his face, and closed his eyes, exhausted by the effort that the words had taken him.

But Milcah stayed up much of the rest of the night, worrying about how to keep her promise. They would not need to pay rent back in Sheffield, so that was a relief at least, but they would need some way to make money to feed them all, and Milcah did not want to think what a return to the air around the mines might do to her siblings.

Then there was the question of actually returning. They still owned the cart that had carried them down to Devon, and Sir Boldheart the mule was still as strong and stubborn as ever, but they were all larger than they had last taken the journey, and her father's condition would make it difficult. She did not know if he would even survive weeks on the road, being jostled by the wheels' every turn. And with him needing to lie down in the bed of the cart, she did not know how all of her younger siblings would fit.

But it was her father's wish—his *dying* wish—and she would do everything she could to honour it.

The solution, in the end, was technology. There was a train station about nine miles away in a town called Axminster, with steam trains that travelled all the way to London.

Once in London, a traveller could then cross the city and find a train back to the North. It would not be as cheap as travelling in a cart and working in exchange for a roof over their heads, and it did not prevent the need to travel on the road entirely, but it would be far quicker and far more comfortable for their father.

So, in the end, Milcah was decided. She and her siblings would set out for the north in the cart, and later, her father, accompanied by Russell, would take the train to follow them. They would spend a night in London, and then continue on their way, making the journey that would take weeks by road in only two or three days. Russell, as the tallest and strongest of the siblings, was deemed the most capable of helping their father if he became tired or unwell, and as Milcah had long since become a mother figure to her youngest siblings, and was the only one with experience driving the cart, it made sense for her to lead the longer journey.

Dale sulked about missing the opportunity to take a real steam train, *hundreds* of miles, but Milcah just smiled sadly and stroked his hair and told him that although it would be a delightful treat, they could not afford tickets for all of them at once. "When you are older, Dale," she said, "and making your own way in the world, then, I promise you, you will ride all the trains you could wish."

Their papa was also nervous about spending so much time away from his children, and especially away from Milcah, but Milcah soothed his worries as well. "You'll have Russell," she said, "and think how exciting it will be. None of us have ever been to London. I can't wait to hear what stories you'll have to tell us once we all reach home."

Grace and Dale both cried to be leaving Devon, and Milcah felt an ache in her heart, too, as she said goodbye to the white cliffs and the brisk sea air. It seemed unlikely that she would ever see them again. But she knew it was what was best for her family, so she packed up the cart, and bid Devon goodbye.

CHAPTER SEVEN

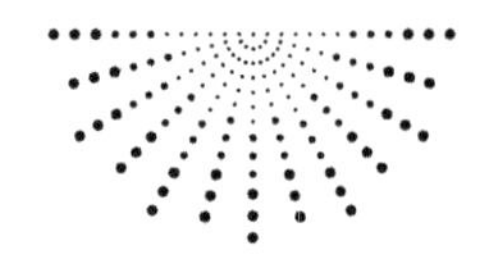

The journey north was as long and hard as the journey south had been several years before, but this time, at least, they were travelling in early summer, with much less rain to fall on their heads. In fact, the largest problem this time was the sun. Milcah insisted that all her siblings wear wide-brimmed hats and cover their arms and legs as much as possible, but even this was not enough to prevent the occasional sunburn. Milcah, for her part driving the cart, was covered by more freckles than she had ever seen on her in her life, and although she knew that the finer folks of England would consider the marks unsightly, she smiled to look at the patterns and constellations that formed across her skin.

Her siblings kept their complaints to a minimum, which Milcah much appreciated, and she tried her best to continue the tradition they had established on their first long journey, encouraging her siblings to play games and tell wild stories. She grew tired of hearing of Jack Rattenbury, the famous smuggler, after Scott told them about him for at least the tenth time, but she delighted to see how creative and inventive her siblings all were, and the weeks passed, if not comfortably, then at least fondly.

But Milcah was still relieved when she saw the familiar smoke stacks in the distance that meant they were approaching Sheffield. The steel factories and their great clouds of smoke thankfully did not extend to their home village of Norton, but the towers stood clear against the horizon as the siblings wove their way across the hills toward the city, and Milcah felt both a pang of homesickness and a pang of horror at the sight of them. Their narrow, smoke-spewing shapes were a deeply familiar sight, reminding her of the home she had not seen for so many years, but they were also partly symbolic of the reason they had all left Sheffield in the first place. The pollution in the air would not be good for any of them. She could only hope that the increased peace of mind it brought her father would have a stronger influence on his health than the smoke and coal dust that would surround them.

From a distance, the village looked much the same as it ever had. It was only as Milcah drove the cart closer that she began to notice the changes. The mines had expanded in their absence, curving around the outside of the village and unleashing more coal dust into the air. Mrs. Smith's old cottage and garden had been replaced with a stable for more pit ponies, and the quiet country road that once ran up to the Foxes' land was worn by the heavy steps of men and horses pulling carts of that black gold. Milcah's heart sank as they made their way to their old home, dreading what they would find there, but it was still a shock when they turned the corner and saw a strange, well-dressed man leaning against the wall of their home, smoking tobacco, while talking to two apparent underlings. More carts and crates lay abandoned around their home, and their land had been partly paved over to allow for easier access.

"What have they done?" Leah gasped, leaning over the side of the cart, but Milcah forced herself to stay calm, even as her hands shook holding the reins. The three men watched their cart approach with idle interest, and Milcah shot a warning glare at her siblings before climbing down from the front seat of the cart to face them. She knew she looked tired and dirty from the long journey, her hair tangled, her skin freckled and her clothes covered in dust, but she stuck up her chin anyway, trying to exude as much confidence as she could.

The man with the tobacco nodded to the other two, and stood up straight as they walked away. He was tall, with the undefined muscles of a man who had once done difficult manual labour but had since found an easier life. He had a thick moustache that had been carefully combed and oiled so that not a single hair lay out of place, a look that contrasted sharply with the food stain on the front of his waistcoat and the scrap of meat she could see stuck in his teeth. He looked at Milcah with unconcerned disdain as she approached.

"This ain't no place for a lady," he said. "Nor for children, neither. I suggest you turn yourself around, miss."

Milcah clenched her fists. "This is our *home.* What are you doing here?"

The man appeared neither surprised nor concerned by her statement. "This?" he said. "This here is property of the Gerald Black Mining Company."

"No," Milcah said, forcing herself to remain calm. "It's our *home.* My father's name is Murray Fox. He owns this house, and the land behind it!"

The man shrugged. "As far as I know, it belongs to the Blacks now. They purchased the mine two years back, and the land came with it. Nobody argued about it, at any rate."

"We were in Devon," Milcah said. "But it's still our land. And we're back!"

The man shrugged. "Now that may be true or it may not be true," he said, "but it ain't got nothing to do with me, I reckon. This here's my office, and I advise you to get moving on, before I get too tired of this conversation."

"We will do no such thing," Milcah said. "This is theft. Where is this Mr. Black? Are you him?"

The man laughed. "I'm the foreman," he said. "Mr. Stentchen to you. The boss isn't here."

"Then when will he be back?"

“I reckon that’s not your concern,” Mr. Stentchen said. “Now get moving. I’ve got work to do.”

“I’m not leaving until you explain yourself,” Milcah said. “This land belongs to *us*.”

“Not any more it doesn’t,” Mr. Stentchen said. “So if you know what’s good fer yer, you’ll get moving, before I have you all done for trespassing.”

“Trespassing!” Milcah cried.

Mr. Stentchen shrugged. “Oi, Trevor! Milkins! Got a job fer yer to do.” The two men who he had been talking to before began to stride back over, and Milcah quickly took in their size and strength, and the apparent unfriendliness in their expressions. The miners had shown no hesitation in threatening or harming her and her sisters before they went to Devon. She had no faith that now would be any different.

She shook with fury as she stared at Mr. Stentchen, and then found herself turning away. He was just the foreman, she told herself. The stupid, petty foreman, with no real power of his own over this issue. She needed to talk to the owner, or perhaps the authorities. She would not fix this here.

Mr. Stentchen jeered at her as she returned to the cart and climbed back onto the front seat.

"What's happening?" Scott said. "Why are we leaving?"

"Just sit tight," Milcah said. "We'll be back before you know it."

"But why?" Scott said. Milcah could think of no easy answer as she pulled on the reins, guiding Sir Boldheart away, so she just shook her head as they made their way back down the road.

"Milcah?" Leah put a comforting hand on Milcah's shoulder. "What happened?"

"The new owners of the mine have *stolen* our land," Milcah said.

"What?" Rachel cried.

"We'll get it back," Milcah said, with more confidence that she felt. "But not by talking to that man. We need to speak to the authorities."

But the authorities were even less help than Mr. Stentchen had been. The constable that Milcah spoke to seemed to have no memory of Milcah or her family, and no desire to correct that lapse. He asked sneeringly if Milcah had a deed for the land or any other proof of ownership, and when Milcah was forced to quietly admit that she did not, he laughed in her face.

"It belonged to my grandfather!" Milcah insisted. "And my great grandfather too. It's not something we *bought*. It's always belonged to us."

"Well, right now it belongs to Mr. Black," the constable said. "Now, I reckon you should go do something useful with yourself, instead of trying to steal scraps of land off your betters."

"It is *our* land," Milcah insisted, but the constable would not listen.

In the end, Milcah was forced to use some of the rest of their savings to rent a small cottage about half a mile away from their home. Thankfully, the landlord was happy to offer a weekly lease and even happier that she wished to move in immediately, but when Milcah considered the ever-shrinking amount in her purse, she knew she had to get their home back soon, or they would find themselves without money or home.

"I will have to speak to the owner," Milcah said to her siblings that evening, as they attempted to settle into their temporary new home. "It may just all be a misunderstanding."

She did not personally believe it. But, given their situation, she had no choice but to make it true.

CHAPTER EIGHT

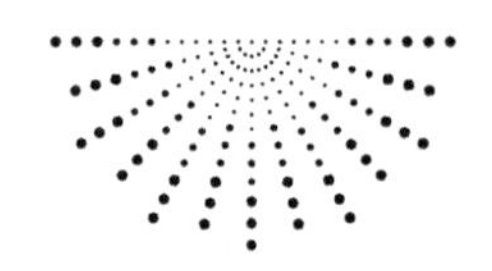

Milcah returned to the foreman's office the next day, and the day after that, each time demanding to know when the mine's owner would return so that she might speak with him in person. Mr. Stentchen by turns laughed at her and threatened her, but she returned day after day, certain that persistence would be the only solution.

On the day that her father's train arrived back in Sheffield, Milcah sent Rachel in the cart to meet him so that she could stay in Norton to question Mr. Stentchen once again. As deeply as Milcah missed her father, she was dreading his reappearance and the moment he learned that their home had been stolen from them. Milcah felt as though she had failed in her duty to him and to her siblings by not recovering the property before he returned, and she worried deeply about the effect that the loss would have on his health. The cottage was not just his home but his father's home, and his grandfather's before that. He would find the loss, even a temporary one, difficult to bear.

But her father faced the news with surprising calmness. He wrapped his arms around Milcah, telling her that he had missed her and thanking her for all her efforts, and then almost immediately went to lie down to recover from the exhaustion of the shock and of the journey.

Milcah refused to give up. She returned to the mines every day, demanding Mr. Stentchen's time and attention. For a while, Mr Stentchen laughed at what he called her pointless persistence, but he quickly grew sick of the sight of her. But Milcah knew she could not stop. Every day, she visited Mr Stentchen's offices, asking after Mr. Black. Every day, Mr. Stentchen dismissed her every question and concern.

But, unbeknownst to Milcah, her efforts began to have an effect. Mr. Stentchen cared no more about helping her on day twenty as he had on day one, but he was growing ever more tired of her presence, and so one day, finally, he wrote to the owner to inform him of the problem.

On the other side of Sheffield, in a grand house the likes of which Milcah had never seen, Gerald Black sat eating breakfast with his son. He was not a particularly tall man, but what he lacked in stature he made up for with sheer force of presence and will. His brown hair was streaked with grey, and his bushy moustache was matched with a pair of fierce, bushy eyebrows, but his face was a kindly one. He sipped his breakfast tea as his son looked through the post that had just been delivered.

"A letter from Mr. Stentchen," his son said idly. "I wonder what he wants now."

Gerald Black's son Leon was twenty-four and taller than his father, but with less of that regal presence that only comes with age and experience. Some might have said that he smiled too much to be truly respected, but Gerald saw the warmth and good humour in his son's heart, and he thanked the boy's now-passed mother for granting him the tools that life had shown Gerald were most necessary for real success and happiness.

"What's the news?" Gerald asked, as his son perused the letter. "Nothing too serious, I hope?"

"The poor man sounds at his wit's end," Leon said. "He complains that a 'wild woman' has been causing him trouble."

"A wild woman?" Gerald repeated with a chuckle.

"Those are his words," Leon said. "He makes it sound like she clambered straight out of the river." Leon read the rest of the letter. "He does not specify more, but he says she is disrupting work and not listening to reason. She's insisting on seeing *you*."

"Strange," Gerald said, "that a *wild woman* would know me by name."

"Mr. Stentchen asks that we visit the mines, if convenient. He thinks our presence may be the only thing to put her off for good."

"I wonder what she wants," Gerald said. "It cannot be work, can it? That could be sorted easily enough."

"Mr. Stentchen can be a curmudgeonly old fool when he wishes," Leon said. "If he's taken a dislike to this woman, he might refuse her employment, no matter how qualified or desperate she was. Still, if all she wants is work, I should be able to solve the problem easily enough."

His father nodded. "Take the carriage down today, then, son," he said. "I can't delay my trip today, but I want it sorted out as soon as we can. I don't want any messy business interrupting things for long."

"Of course, father," Leon said. "I'll go at once."

At the Fox cottage, Milcah was attempting to cheer both herself and her family with some morning porridge. Mr. Stentchen had taken to avoiding her visits entirely over the past several days, and even though the building was technically her property, Milcah knew things would escalate and the police would be called if she tried to enter his supposed office without permission. But *something* needed to change.

She considered her father. He was still somewhat tired from the journey, but his mind seemed sharp this morning, as he entertained Russell and Dale about old Roman ghosts in the mines. How the Romans got into the mines, which were only constructed in the past hundred years, Milcah did not know, and she did not want to ruin the fun by asking, as Dale looked captivated by the dangers of the tale.

"Well, papa," she said, once they hit a lull in the story, "perhaps you could see if you can find any above ground today." Her father raised an eyebrow at her, and she forced herself to smile. "I think it would be good if Mr. Stentchen were to meet you. He just thinks I'm a foolish girl, I'm sure. Your presence might help."

"I doubt I'd add much force to the argument," her father said. Milcah secretly agreed. Although she did not wish to say as such in front of her father, she imagined that her father's assistance would be more in the realm of inspiring pity than respect. The foreman had shown very little sign of having human feelings so far, but Milcah knew that he must have some goodness and charity in his heart, and she hoped that the sight of her struggling father might be enough to convince him that they truly needed their land returned to them, and inspire him to at least contact Mr. Black.

Milcah and her father travelled together on the front bench of the cart. Milcah placed a blanket over her father's legs out of fear of a Northern late-summer chill, but her father seemed perfectly comfortable as the cart rattled its way along the half mile to their old home. When their cottage came into view, her father stared at it without speaking, and the wistfulness that she saw in his eyes only confirmed her need to win this fight.

Mr. Stentchen was smoking outside the front door as they approached. Milcah half expected him to turn directly around and slam the door behind him on his way inside, as he had the last time she had seen him, but either he was in a better mood or he was enjoying his tobacco too much to waste it, because this time he just watched them approach with a slight smirk on his face.

"Good morning, Mr. Stentchen," Milcah said, as she pulled Sir Boldheart to a stop and began to climb down from the cart.

"Good morning to you too, miss," he said. "I see you've brought a guest with you today."

"Yes," Milcah said. "Mr. Stentchen, this is my father, Murray Fox. The rightful owner of this land." She held up a hand to her father and helped him carefully descend from the bench. She felt Mr. Stentchen watching them. "Father, this is Mr. Stentchen, the foreman of the mines."

"How do you do?" her father said with a slight bow, once he was safely on solid ground again.

Mr Stentchen laughed. "If this is a new attempt to move me, Miss Fox, you'll be disappointed."

"It is not an attempt for anything except justice," Milcah said. "This land belongs to my family, and to my father most of all. I thought you might like to meet the man you are helping to rob."

Mr. Stentchen spat on the ground. "You don't give up, girl, I'll give you that. Well, might be I actually have news for you, if you care to hear it. I wrote to the owner, just like you requested."

"You did?" Milcah asked. She was momentarily stunned. It was what she'd hoped for, but she had not actually expected it to happen, or at least not so soon.

"I did," Mr. Stentchen confirmed. "I told him how a wild girl kept showing up at my office, disrupting work. Suggested he might want to do something about it. So you can quit asking me."

"That's not what I asked you to tell him!" Milcah said.

He laughed. "It's the truth though, ain't it? Now, if you're lucky, he'll do nothing about it. But if *I'm* lucky, he'll be around here sooner rather than later and he'll put an end to your meddling for good."

"Are you threatening my daughter, sir?" Murray asked. He shook slightly on his bad leg, and put a hand on Milcah's shoulder to hold himself steady.

"No threat," Mr. Stentchen said. "Just the truth. You've still got a chance to leave, girl. If you know what's good for you, you will."

"No," Milcah said. "Thank you for writing to Mr. Black. I look forward to meeting him."

Mr. Stentchen shook his head with a disparaging laugh and moved to walk back into his office. Milcah, strengthened by the promise of Mr. Black's appearance, helped her father to sit and then settled down to wait.

They did not have to wait long. Soon, a grand, expensive-looking carriage appeared at the end of the road. The sleek wood and curtained windows looked completely out of place among the coal dust of Norton, and Milcah found herself thinking, perhaps irrationally, that it was lucky the carriage horses were black, as otherwise the air here would mar their beautiful coats.

The carriage driver pulled the horses to a stop directly in front of Milcah and her father, and a moment later, a tall, well-dressed man stepped out. He looked a few years older than Milcah, with neatly combed dark hair and a surprisingly open face for one who appeared so rich. For a moment, Milcah was certain that she recognised him. His features looked so familiar. But who of her acquaintance could possibly be so rich? She frowned at him, struggling to place him. No, she thought, after a moment. Whoever she was remembering, this man was not them. It was a passing resemblance to a face she had once seen, that was all.

The stranger looked around a little uncertainly, and Milcah took her chance. She stood and marched over to him.

"Mr. Gerald Black?" she asked.

The man blinked at her in surprise. "Leon Black," he corrected, after a moment. "Gerald Black is my father."

"But you speak for him?" Milcah pressed. "You speak for his business?"

"I do," Leon said. He frowned at her. "May I ask who you are?"

"My name is Milcah Fox," she said. "And this is my family's land that we are standing on. Now I suggest you give it back to us, or—"

The door to their old house opened, interrupting her, and Mr. Stentchen stepped out. "My apologies, sir," Mr. Stentchen said. His voice took on an oily tone that Milcah had never heard from him before. "I see you've already met the wild girl I told you about."

"I am not a *wild girl—*" Milcah interrupted, but he ignored her.

"Here every day, she is, sir, making demands, disrupting work. A menace, she is. Now I don't want to put my hands on a lady, nor on her crippled father neither, but she's got to be dealt with."

"Hmm," Leon said. He gave Mr. Stentchen a long, considering look. "And you're unable to deal with her demands? Isn't that part of what we pay you for?"

"She's back every day, sir," Mr. Stentchen said. "Like an infestation, she is. You never can quite get rid of her."

"I cannot be an infestation on my own land!" Milcah said. "Mr. Black, perhaps you were unaware when you expanded this mine, but this building and this land belong to my family, as they have for generations. We left Norton for a short while, but we never sold the land to anybody, and your use of it is *theft*. As you can see, Mr. Black, my father is not well. We need our home back."

Leon frowned at her. "You claim this land belongs to you?"

"It's not a claim, sir!" Milcah said. "It's a fact. I'm certain you understand that buildings and pieces of land are not available for you to take, simply because the owner is absent for a short while."

"This a serious accusation indeed," Leon said. "But without proof, I'm afraid I cannot give up this land to you. This mine means a great deal to my father."

"As a *business,*" Milcah said. "You think your father's business interests are more important than my family's whole livelihood? Build the office somewhere else! Buy other land!"

"This land is in the middle of our property," Leon said. "But I am not unfeeling, Miss Fox. Your family is clearly in need of help. I promise I will do everything in my power to make sure you and your family are well cared for."

"*Well cared for?*" Milcah repeated. "We don't need caring for, Mr Black. We need what is rightfully ours."

"The girl is just a nuisance, sir," Mr. Stentchen said. "If you give her anything, others'll follow her."

"I won't have it said I've done harm—"

"You won't have it *said* you've done harm. You don't mind actually doing it," Milcah said. "I am not asking for charity or for pity! I am asking for what rightfully belongs to us."

"Milcah, please," her father said, putting a hand on her arm. "Calm down."

"I will not," Milcah said. "This man stands here and speaks about *caring* for us, as though he's not the one who stole from us in the first place. You are a selfish, heartless man, sir," she said to Leon, "and I won't accept your pity. I'll only accept what we're rightly owed."

Leon looked nervously between Milcah and Mr. Stentchen. "I will do what I can, Miss Fox," he said, "but I don't know what *can* be done. I will speak to my father on the matter, but—"

"Speak to him, then!" Milcah said. "I won't stop coming here until I can speak to him myself."

"Milcah…" her father moaned. He grasped her arm, fighting to hold himself upright, but he was not strong enough, and he collapsed to the ground.

"Papa!" Milcah knelt down beside him. "What's the matter?"

"I am just tired, my dear," he said. "Just tired, that's all." He tried to stand, but collapsed again.

"Here, papa," Milcah said. She tried to help him to his feet, but his good leg would not support his weight, and he stumbled again. Leon darted forward, reaching out to help, and Milcah turned on him with a snarl. "I told you we don't require your help or your charity," she said.

Leon put his hands up in surrender and stepped away as Milcah continued to try and haul her father to his feet. Tears burned in her eyes, the fear and frustration of the past several weeks overwhelming her as she saw herself failing to help her father with this one simple thing. She could not get their house back; she could not even help him stand when he was weak.

She put all her strength into hauling him upwards and wrapping his arm around her shoulder to support him, and for a moment, it worked. Then she tried to take a step, and her father gasped in pain and slipped. Milcah desperately tried to grab him as he fell, but she was not strong enough, and he crashed to his knees.

"I'm sorry, papa," Milcah said. She got down onto her knees beside him, but what little strength she'd had in her arms was gone, and she was terrified of hurting her father even more by letting him slip again.

Burning with frustration and humiliation, Milcah turned to look at Leon Black. He was still standing a few feet away, watching the scene, and the moment he saw her imploring face, he smiled gently. Milcah thought the kindness in his face might almost be worse than disdain after all that had happened.

"May I?" he asked.

Milcah nodded and scrambled out of the way as Leon strode forwards and picked up her father in his arms as though he weighed no more than Milcah did.

"The cart," Milcah said, in a hoarse voice. "If you could please put him in the cart, so I can take him home—"

"I would rather take him in my carriage," Leon said, "if you will allow me. He will be more comfortable, and I don't want to jolt his leg any more than necessary on the journey."

Milcah opened her mouth to argue again, but then she saw how pale her father's face was, and she forced herself to nod instead. It stung her pride to have this rich man help them, but she could not hurt her father for the sake of her own pride.

Leon carried her father into his carriage, and instructed his driver to follow Milcah home. He hesitated at his own carriage door, looking at her as though wondering whether he should approach her again, but then seemed to think better of it, and climbed inside after her father.

Milcah drove the cart home alone, with nothing to distract her from the nagging worry in her stomach over her father's health and her own inability to help him. It irked her, more than she could express, that this stranger, this rich man who could turn all of their fortunes around, would act so kind and generous in all ways but the way that she needed. They did not need the charity of the rich, she thought furiously, as she steered Sir Boldheart down the lane toward their cottage. They just needed what was rightfully theirs.

Her siblings came running at the sound of *two* vehicles arriving outside the front door, and they gasped and gaped as they saw Leon

Black's sleek carriage and shining black horses.

"Milcah! Milcah!" Dale shouted, running up to her and almost scrambling into the cart with excitement. "Who's that, Milcah? Whose carriage is that?"

"Hush, now," Milcah said, as she climbed down from the seat and unfastened the reins. "He's a guest from the mines."

Leon's carriage door opened, and Leon stepped out, before turning back and helping her still shaky-looking father down the steps.

"Papa!" Leah ran forward. "Is he all right?"

"He will be," Leon said kindly. "He just needs a little rest." Leah moved to try and take her father's weight, but Leon shook his head and began to help lead him inside.

Milcah gritted her teeth. "Dale," she said. "Unhitch Sir Boldheart and make sure he's taken care of."

"But *Milcah*," he whined. "I want to meet the stranger!"

"Please," Milcah said. "For me." She handed Sir Boldheart's reins to her brother and hurried after Leon.

His clothes and demeanour looked even finer inside their raggedy cottage, and Milcah wiped her hands on her skirt self-consciously, wondering just what exactly this rich man must think of them. But it didn't matter, she reminded herself, as she watched Leon help her father into his chair. She did not care what this man thought of them.

"What's your name, sir?" Rachel asked, grinning at him.

"My name is Leon Black," Leon said, with a little bow that made Rachel and Leah both giggle. "My father owns the mines around here."

"Thank you for your assistance, Mr. Black," Milcah said stiffly, but Rachel interrupted her.

"Do you live in Norton, Mr. Black?"

"No, sadly I do not," Leon said. "I live in a village about four miles away."

"Why did you come all this way?" she asked.

"Well, my foreman told me that a very interesting girl kept coming to the mines," he said, with a glance at Milcah, "and I wanted to see her for myself."

"Mr Black! Mr Black!" Little Grace ran up to him. "Did you know the mines are *haunted*?"

Milcah wanted to cover her face from embarrassment, but Leon just smiled. "I did not know that," he said.

Grace nodded gravely. "Papa told us," she said. "A whole battalion of Roman soldiers walk the mines at night, looking for the road home. But they never find it, because they're in a *mine*. And then there's a Wailing Woman, who—"

"That's enough, Grace," Milcah said.

But Leon was still smiling. "The Wailing Woman?" he asked.

Grace seemed slightly cowed by Milcah's admonishment, but Russell was more than happy to take up the story. "Her husband went missing down the mines," he said, "and she wandered in after him to try and find him, but she didn't know the mines at all, and once her light went out, she was lost in the darkness. So she wanders the mines in the dark, calling for her husband and crying out for help, for all of eternity!"

"Papa didn't tell you that one," Milcah said. Her father's stories were never actually frightening.

"I heard it elsewhere," Russell said with a shrug. He glanced at Scott as he did so, and Milcah immediately understood exactly who the source had been.

"Clearly, I should have done my research," Leon said.

Grace nodded seriously. "You've always got to watch out for the ghosts, Mr. Black," she said. "Cos they can work with you, or they can work against you, depending on how you treat 'em and how they look at you. My pa says we should always be kind in everything we do, because we don't know what people have suffered, including spirits, and good deeds always come back to us, but bad ones come back worse."

"Your pa is a wise man," Leon said.

Murray chuckled from his chair. A little of the colour was returning to his face.

Leah and Rachel were whispering to each other, blushing slightly as they looked at Leon, and then Rachel stepped forward boldly. "Would you like to stay for dinner, Mr. Black?" she said. "My sister Milcah is an amazing cook."

Milcah took in her sisters' blushes and Rachel's bold smile, and she had to fight back a frustrated sigh. Of *course,* her sisters would find Mr. Black handsome. They saw so few young men, and even fewer that were as rich and well-dressed as this one.

"Mr. Black is far too busy to have dinner with the likes of us, Rachel," she said. "Hush now."

"I'm afraid I do have another engagement this evening," Leon said, with a smile. "But how about Friday? Would that be amenable?"

Milcah stared at him, utterly speechless, as Rachel and Leah giggled. "Yes," Rachel said boldly. "That would be amenable. Wouldn't it, Milcah?"

Everyone turned to look at Milcah, and she could have sworn that Leon looked amused behind his polite smile. Was he mocking her? She wouldn't back down if he was.

"All right," she said, a little less graciously than she would have hoped. "Friday dinner."

Leon beamed. He looked so happy, in fact, that Milcah had to look away, lest her dislike of the man soften too much.

"I look forward to it," Leon said. "Now I don't wish to be rude, but if you will forgive me, I need to move on and complete some other business for my father. But it was a pleasure to meet you all."

"You too!" Leah said, peering around her sister, and then immediately blushed scarlet. Murray laughed.

"Thank you so much for your help, Mr. Black," he said. "We truly appreciate it." He tried to stand, but Leon hurried over to him and put a gentle hand on his shoulder, encouraging him to remain seated.

"I am glad to have been some small help," Leon said. He bowed, and Milcah forced herself to walk with him to the door and see him out.

"Thank you," she said quietly, as much as she resented it, "for helping my father."

"Of course," Leon said. "What sort of man would I be if I didn't?" When they reached the door, he put his hand in his pocket and pulled out a wallet. "I want to give you some money," he said, "for medicine for your father. And for dinner on Friday, as well. I know you weren't planning for a guest."

"No," Milcah said stiffly. "Thank you, but no. We don't need any money. But thank you for your help."

Leon hesitated and then nodded. "Until Friday, then, Miss Fox," he said.

Milcah watched him leave without another word.

Later, they found several bank notes tucked under a stone directly outside the front door. Milcah grumbled at the man's stubborn audacity, but even she had to admit that she was surprised at his kindness, and the medicine the money bought did her father a world of good.

CHAPTER NINE

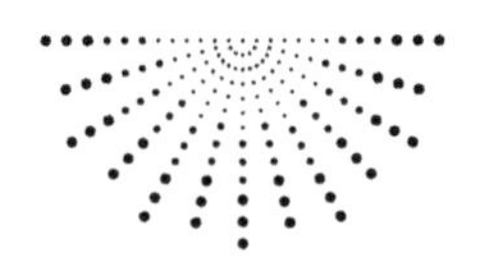

The following morning, Milcah walked down to the foreman's office, as she always did, to demand again that she be allowed to speak to Gerald Black. She expected a morning of arguing with the foreman, at the very best, and was surprised when she approached to see Leon Black stepping out of the office door.

What on earth could he have been talking to the foreman about, she wondered. Had he returned to plot ways to get rid of her after all? But when Leon saw her, he gave her a sincere-looking smile and bowed in greeting.

"Good morning, Miss Fox," he said.

"Good morning, Mr Black. What brings you back here again?"

"Well," Leon said. He walked closer to her, stopping about an arm's reach away. "Yesterday made me realise that I don't know enough about the day-to-day running of the mines. My father purchased this operation to do some good and improve the conditions that the workers find themselves in. But how can we claim to do that when we're rarely here ourselves?"

"You bought the mine to do good?" Milcah repeated. She could not stop herself from raising her eyebrows skeptically. "A *mine*."

"Yes," Leon said, sounding a little surprised by her cynicism. "The mines are necessary. Coal is vital for everything this great nation has achieved these past decades and everything we will achieve going forward. It is vital to improve all of our lives, and to increase prosperity here in the North as well. But that should not mean that so many have to be injured or killed while mining it. My father has instituted new rules and regulations, working hour limits, a minimum age, safety protocols and payments for those who are tragically hurt. He may be rich, Miss Fox, but he is not an unfeeling man. He wishes to make a difference. And so do I. No more stories like your brother's Wailing Woman."

He gave her a good-natured smile, like they were sharing a secret joke together, and Milcah fought the urge to smile back. His words were difficult to believe, but he seemed genuine, and the fact threw her.

"That's… good of you," Milcah said eventually. "If it's true."

"I hope it is true," Leon said. "I do all that I can to ensure that it is. But if there are problems, such as the one that you're having, I wish to hear about them and address them."

Milcah scowled at him. "Yes, you are so kindly refusing to return our land to us. Truly, the generosity is astounding."

Leon winced. "It is more complicated than that," he said. "The land belongs to my father, and without a deed of ownership from yourself—"

"You are newcomers here," Milcah said. "Everyone knows this land belongs to us. You are being kind to try and soothe your guilt, but you are still a thief, Leon Black."

Leon nodded. "Then I will give you some peace, Miss Fox," he said. "Good day to you."

Milcah watched him leave, anger stewing inside her. How dare this man act like he and his father were generous, charitably folks, after stealing from them? She could not stand the falseness of it.

But, she found herself thinking, throughout the rest of the day, Leon Black's goal was a noble one, if he was telling her the truth. It could not prevent the bad air from harming the little ones' lungs, but with most of the money in the area coming from work in the mines, it would be no small thing for conditions to improve. Fewer families would lose loved ones if the owners cared more about safety than about profit, and if Leon was telling the truth about paying compensation to workers who were injured at work, then that would make all the difference to suffering families. Milcah could not imagine how different things would have been if her father's employer had not thrown him aside the moment he was too injured to work.

She even asked Mr. Stentchen about the issue. He rolled his eyes at her nosiness, but seemed almost pleased to have something new to rant about around her. "We make half as much money as we used to," he said. "Get half as much coal and spend far too much of our profits on paying for things for the workers. It's a waste, if you ask me. Not that anyone ever does. People are here to work, not to be coddled by the miner owner."

But Mr. Stentchen's sincere frustration with Mr. Black was enough to make Milcah believe that Leon had been telling the truth.

She was surprised to see him the next day too, walking down the lane. "Good afternoon, Miss Fox," he called to her, with a tip of his hat.

"Good afternoon, Mr Black," she replied.

"How is your father?" Leon asked, as he drew closer.

"As well as can be expected," Milcah said. "Thank you." They both paused for a moment, considering one another.

"Mr. Stetchen tells me you've been asking about me," Leon said, with a good-natured smile.

Milcah stuck up her chin, refusing to be cowed. "I did," she said. "I wanted to know if what you told me was true."

"And what's the verdict?"

"You annoy Mr. Stentchen," she said. "So I suppose you must be doing something right."

Leon laughed, and Milcah could not resist smiling slightly in return. "I'm glad to hear it," he said.

Then Milcah frowned. She could not allow herself to forget the issue between them, just because he had a pleasant smile. "Mr. Black, have you had chance to speak with your father about our problem yet? I would very much like to meet him to discuss it."

"I'm afraid not, Miss Fox," he said. "My father is away in York for the week on business. He's not expected back until Monday."

"And you are completely powerless without his say-so?"

Leon sighed. "Please, Miss Fox. Will you allow me to cover the rent in your cottage for this week? It is partly my fault that you are having to wait for an answer, because I do not have the authority myself. Allow me to ease that burden, at least."

"No, thank you, Mr Black," Milcah said. "We are perfectly capable of taking care of ourselves. But I look forward to Monday then."

"Is the invitation to dinner on Friday still open?" he asked, with a hesitant smile. "Or would you prefer not to see me until my father returns?"

"I am sure you have better things to do with your Friday evening than spending it with my family," Milcah said. "It was kind of you to appease my sister like that, but I rather assumed you would not actually come."

"I won't if I am not welcome," Leon said. "But I was rather looking forward to it. Your sister says you are an excellent cook, and I have to admit, I would enjoy the company greatly."

Milcah felt herself blushing, and looked away. "Well, then," she said. "Of course, you are welcome, if you would like to be."

"Then I would love to come," he said.

That night, Milcah found herself spending far too much time thinking about what to prepare for Friday's dinner. They still had a little of Leon's money left over after buying her father medicine, and she had to admit that she was excited to be able to create something without being limited to her usual sparse ingredients. Perhaps, she thought, she would even buy fish. She doubted Leon would ever have met anyone with such expertise preparing it as she had, after their years in Beer.

But, she told herself, as she washed up the dishes that night, she was not trying to *impress* Leon Black. She was excited by the opportunity to cook with better ingredients, and she needed to convince Leon to support her and her family against his father, but that was all. There was nothing personal about the meal at all.

The next day, she encountered Leon Black again, as she walked down the lane and she saw him speaking with one of the workers.

Milcah did not want to interrupt him, but a few minutes later, she heard hurried footsteps on the road behind her, and she turned to see Leon half-running towards her.

"Miss Fox," he said.

"Mr. Black," she replied. "Is something the matter?"

"Oh," he said, and he blushed slightly. "No, nothing is wrong. I just did not want you to pass by without speaking with you. I thought it would be rude."

"You were occupied," Milcah said, but she could not quite stop herself from smiling. "It seemed important."

Leon nodded. He seemed almost at a loss about what to say. "Ah," he said finally. "I was wondering what time for dinner tomorrow. Is seven a good time?"

"Seven would be perfect," Milcah said.

"Excellent." He nodded again. "Give my regards to your father, then. And—yes. I hope he is still doing well. And you as well, Miss Fox, of course."

"He is," she said with a smile. "And I am."

"Very well," Leon said. "I'm glad to hear it. Well, I'll see you tomorrow, if you'll excuse me—"

Still blushing slightly, he gave her another little bow and turned to walk away.

"Mr Black," Milcah said, and he paused and looked back. "I just wanted to say—thank you, sir, for your kindness to my father. The past few years have been very difficult for him, and we have been unable to give him all the help that we wished. The medicine we got eases the aches in his limbs, and I know it's a great relief to him. It's a great relief to me as well."

Leon bowed again. "Of course, Miss Fox," he said. "Anything I can do—please. You only have to ask."

He lingered another moment, seeming uncertain of what to do next. When Milcah could not think of anything else to say, he bowed again and took his leave.

Milcah watched him go, unable to stop herself from smiling.

CHAPTER TEN

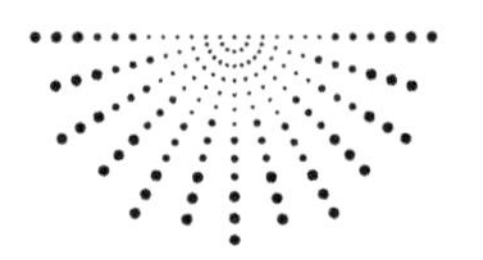

The Fox house was in chaos in the hours before Leon Black arrived for dinner. Dale and Grace ran around, full of excitement for the guest, and the older siblings were not much better. Leah and Rachel giggled together as they adjusted their dresses and primped their hair, determined to look as fine as possible for their rich and handsome dinner guest. Milcah had to bite her lip to stop herself from laughing when she saw the twins pinching one another's cheeks to create a healthy blush.

Milcah did not have time for such distractions. The funds that Leon had provided allowed her to purchase some of the finest ingredients she had ever cooked with, and she was determined to do them justice. This meal would be a feast for all of them to remember, but especially Leon. She wanted him to see what a poor girl—a *wild woman,* as the foreman had called her—was capable of. She wanted his first bite of the meal to stun him beyond any of his expectations.

Still, she found herself adjusting her hair slightly in her reflection in the metal part of the oven. It would not hurt to present a neat exterior to their guest, after all.

At seven o'clock, they heard an approaching carriage through the window, and Milcah had to grab her sister Grace to prevent her from running straight outside to accost their guest. A knock sounded at the front door a few moments later, and Milcah straightened her skirts and readjusted one final hairpin before crossing the room to answer it.

Leon Black looked particularly tall in the doorway. He was wearing a fine suit, as always, with his hat in his hands, but his dark hair was slightly messy, as though he had been running his fingers through it nervously not a moment before. He bowed when he saw Milcah, a bright smile spreading across his face.

"Good evening, Miss Fox," he said. "Mr. Fox."

Rachel barreled forward, almost falling over her own feet in her haste. "Good evening, Mr Black," she said. "Welcome to our home."

Leon and Milcah shared an amused look as Leon stepped inside. He removed his coat and hat, and then, before Milcah could close the door, leant back outside and picked up a covered pot.

"What's that?" Grace asked. "Is it for us?"

"*Grace,*" Milcah said in warning, but Leon just laughed.

"It certainly is," he said. "I couldn't allow your sister to do all the hard work and show up empty handed. This is a dessert for all of us."

"Dessert?" Grace repeated, her eyes going wide. "What is it?"

"You'll have to wait and see," Leon said. "We have your sister's feast to enjoy first, and I'm certain this will pale in comparison to what she's got prepared."

"She didn't make dessert," Dale said. "She *never* makes dessert."

"Dale, hush," Milcah said. She felt herself blushing. She did all that she could to prepare good food for her family, but their budget never extended to such luxuries as sugar. They had all eaten cakes and sweets on a few rare occasions in their lives, but the idea of having an entire dessert between them at home on a normal Friday evening was almost unimaginable. Milcah felt a little spark of annoyance that Leon was still giving them *charity,* but when she saw the joy on her siblings' faces, and the sincere smile on Leon's as he waited for her reaction, she found that she was more grateful than perturbed.

"Thank you, Mr. Black," she said, after a moment. She held out her hands to take it. "I'll put it in the kitchen until it's time." As she took the dish off him, her fingers brushed his. It was only the briefest of touches, barely worthy of notice, but Milcah's skin tingled, and her heart beat faster all the same.

They all settled around the dining table, with Leon taking pride of place next to Milcah's father and Milcah sitting opposite him. For a few minutes, the family fell quiet as they all savoured the meal that Milcah had prepared. The ingredients, Milcah thought, really did make all the difference. She had made similar things many times before, but they had never tasted quite so rich and rewarding before.

"Mr Black," her father finally said. "My daughter tells me you don't live in Norton. Are you from Sheffield originally?"

Leon nodded. "My family are actually from Meersbrook," he said, naming a village that was only a couple of miles away, and a little closer to Sheffield itself. "I grew up there with my mother and father and my siblings. But we moved about nine or ten years ago."

"And are your siblings all involved in the coal business?" Murray asked.

"Unfortunately not," Leon said. "I'm afraid my mother and my siblings all died of an illness several years back. It was the reason we left Meersbrook, I believe, although I was too young to fully understand it at the time."

"My condolences," Murray said. "Such a thing must have been very hard on the family."

"It was," Leon said. "But there is good in bad. It had a great effect on my father. Ever since, he has been working to better people's lives. That is why he purchased the mine. I only hope I can continue his example."

"That is a noble cause," Murray said. He glanced at Milcah, as though gauging her reaction.

"Thank you, sir," Leon said. He took another bite of the fish. "Your sister was right, Miss Fox," he added. "This is truly delicious."

"Thank you," Milcah said quietly.

"You have an impressive daughter, Mr. Fox," Leon continued. "Her determination and her dedication to her family are truly admirable."

Milcah felt herself blushing. She looked down at her plate, concentrating on her next bite, while her father smiled. "That's kind of you to say, sir," he said. "We certainly all believe so. She's kept us going through the dark times. What more could you hope for from a daughter?"

Now Leon turned to Milcah. "Miss Fox," he said. "I swear to you, when my father returns, I will do everything I can to help you get your land back."

"Thank you," Milcah said again, warmth growing in her heart. She looked up, meeting Leon's gaze, and was surprised by how fond and caring it looked. "That is all I ask."

The evening continued with the younger children peppering Leon with questions, and although Milcah tried to hush them once more, Leon only laughed, seeming more than happy to answer their curiosity. The children, for their part, told Leon about Sir Boldheart—both the knight and the mule—and hounded him for ghost stories until he told them about every strange thing that had ever happened in his house, and Scott declared severely that it sounded like "a proper haunting."

The time for dessert came, and Leon pulled back the cover on his dish to reveal an Apple Charlotte, a treat that none of the siblings had eaten before but that Leon assured them was the height of both fashion and deliciousness. The children devoured the concoction of apple, cake and custard so quickly that Milcah would have apologised for their manners if

Leon had not seemed delighted by their enthusiasm. When Milcah took her first bite of the dessert, she could not stop the large smile from spreading across her face. It was the perfect mix of sweetness and tartness, and when she looked up from the dish, she saw Leon watching her, beaming at her reaction.

The younger ones were reluctant to go to bed that night, but Murray eventually shepherded them away with the promise of a story, leaving Milcah alone with Leon. She began to tidy up the plates and carry them over to the sink, and she was surprised and delighted when Leon strode over to help her.

"There's no need for that," Milcah said. "You're our guest."

"You cooked the best meal I've eaten in a very long time," Leon said. "The least I can do is help you clean up." He collected the remaining plates from the table and smiled at her as he placed them in the sink.

"Thank you," she said. Then she couldn't help adding: "I don't imagine you need to do much cleaning or chores, growing up rich. You probably have servants to do it all for you."

"We do," Leon admitted. "But my father is not fond of laziness in any man, and especially not his son. The servants are there to help with the running of the house, not to take all the responsibility and labour on themselves."

"I imagine that is an unusual perspective," Milcah said.

"I hope it is not," Leon said. "But do you mean you think it a bad thing?"

"No," Milcah said softly. "Not at all." She did not know what else to say, so she began to scrub the dishes.

"Miss Fox," Leon said. "I hope you know that you are the most amazing woman I have ever met."

Milcah froze and turned to look at him with wide eyes.

"That face suggests to me that you did not know," Leon said gently. "But I promise you that it's true."

"I don't know what you mean," Milcah said quickly. "Just because I can cook a good meal doesn't mean that—"

"That is not what I am talking about," Leon said, "and I think you know that. You are wonderful, Miss Fox. I hope one day you will allow me to tell you so."

"You—you can say whatever you please," Milcah said. She could feel her whole face burning, and her heart was beating fast. She could not look at him.

"Well, then I hope one day you will believe me," Leon said. He smiled and stepped back. "I have taken up too much of your time and hospitality. Thank you again for the delicious meal. I hope we may share another one again soon."

Reaching forward, he took her hand in his and brought it up to his lips. A thrill ran across the back of Milcah's hand, and her breath caught in her throat as he held her hand for a long moment, smiling kindly at her.

Then he bowed at her and took his leave. Milcah found herself staring at the door where he had departed, long after he was gone.

CHAPTER ELEVEN

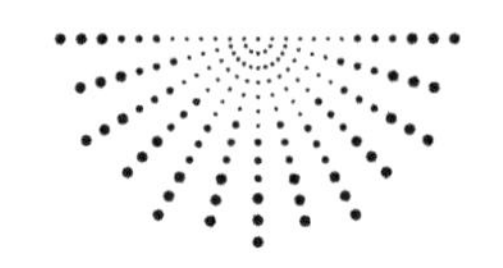

The following morning, Milcah was preparing for her usual trip to visit Mr. Stentchen when her father approached her.

"I think I should like to join you today, my dear, if that's all right," he said.

"You wish to speak to Mr. Stentchen?" she asked.

He laughed and shook his head. "I want to thank Mr. Black in person again for his visit."

"There's no guarantee Mr. Black will be there," Milcah said, blushing slightly. "He often isn't."

"It sounds to me," her father said, "that he's been there every day since he met you. I reckon if I stay by your side, I'll come across him soon enough."

"What are you implying, papa?" Milcah asked him.

"What he implied himself last night," he replied. "He seems rather besotted with you."

Milcah felt herself blushing harder, but she shook her head. "I don't think that's true, papa," she said softly.

"Now, then," her father said, "I didn't raise a fool, now, did I? We both know that's what he was implying. Only question is how *you* feel about him."

Milcah shook her head. "It's silly," she said. "Even if he *did* care for me—and I'm not convinced that he does, but if he *did*—nothing would come of it. He's a rich tradesman, a mine owner, and I'm just—"

"The cook of the most delicious meal he had ever eaten?" her father said with a laugh. "Someone he calls *truly admirable*?"

"Hush, papa," Milcah said. "He was just being polite."

But her heart was skipping with excitement as she and her father made their way toward Mr. Stentchen's office, and she could not quite suppress her smile of delight when she saw Leon's carriage parked just outside it.

"Strange," her father said, when he spotted it as well. "Who could have expected that?" He laughed, and Milcah ducked her head away, blushing.

They climbed down from the front of their cart and began to slowly make their way to the door. Before they got there, however, they heard the sound of another carriage approaching on the road. When they turned to look, they saw a sleek, grand-looking carriage, complete with coachman and pulled by a dappled horse. It pulled off the road, and the coachman leapt down from his seat to open the carriage door. A moment later, an older-looking gentleman dressed in fine clothes stepped out.

His face was immediately, intimately familiar to Milcah. He certainly resembled Leon, in a way that suggested they were closely related, but that was not where the familiarity ended. She again felt the strong sensation that she had seen this face—this exact face—somewhere before, but time had blurred her memory, and she could not recall precisely where.

Behind her, she heard someone step out of the building, and turned to see Leon striding towards the newcomer with his hand outstretched. The men shook hands, and the newcomer clapped Leon on the back familiarly.

"Father!" Leon said. "I wasn't expecting you until Monday."

"Well, after the letter you sent me last night," he said, "I couldn't wait another day. Is this the girl?"

"Yes," Leon said, grinning. "Father, allow me to introduce Miss Milcah Fox and her father, Mr. Murray Fox. Miss Fox, Mr. Fox, this is my father, Gerald Black."

"It's a pleasure to meet you," Mr. Black said. He shook Milcah's hand vigorously, and then turned to her father. Then he paused, as though in shock.

"Father?" Leon asked. "Is everything all right?"

Mr. Black's blank, shocked expression melted into a broad, delighted grin. "Things are more than all right, son," he said. "Leon, this man and his family who saved my life, over eight years ago now."

Leon's eyes grew wide in understanding, but Milcah frowned, trying to figure out what on earth the man could mean. Then, all at once, she remembered. "The man my father found in the river," she gasped. "The one we took care of."

"The very same," Mr. Black said. He shook Murray's hand vigorously, and then turned back to Milcah and took her hand again. "You must be the eldest daughter, the wonderful cook who gave me my strength back. You've grown so much."

"You left," Milcah gasped, not knowing what to say. "One morning, you were gone."

"I felt guilty, Miss Fox," he said. "Guilty that such a poor family could give so much to me. I heard you speaking to the little ones, telling them I might be an angel, and I was certainly no angel at the time, but you treated me as such. I was so ashamed of who I was, and of receiving your help when I could not possibly deserve it, that I snuck out as soon as I could. I did not want you to find out the truth of who I was."

"Kindness is not earned," Murray said. "All manner of men deserve it."

"Wise words," Mr. Black said, "and a sentiment that your family taught me. You had so little, and had suffered so much loss, yet you were so full of kindness and joy, even toward me, a complete stranger who believed he did not deserve a single drop of love or sympathy. You changed everything for me that day."

"But you're rich," Milcah said, and then immediately felt silly for saying so. Still, it seemed impossible that a rich mine owner's life could have been changed by a bed in a small cottage and a little inexpertly prepared broth.

"Yes," Mr. Black said. "I was then as well, richer even, but it did me no good. I was greedy and selfish, always putting the pursuit of money above the care of my own family. And then the sickness came and took my dear wife and five of my little ones away, all in the space of days. Leon fell ill too, and I felt certain he would die. I thought they had all suffered for my sins, that God saw I did not value my family and so saw fit to take them away."

"But how did you end up in the river?" Milcah asked.

Mr. Black sighed. "I could not bear all the loss and the guilt," he said. "I travelled one village over to Norton to end my life. But like a gift from God, your father saw me and rescued me, even though I did not deserve it. At the time, I almost wished that he had left me, as broken and confused as I was. But when I saw the kindness that you all shared, and the peace and faith in your hearts, I began to see how wrong I had been. I did not want to leave this life, when there was a great deal left that I might do to improve it. When I returned home, I discovered that Leon had survived, by God's grace. We were both spared, allowed to remain on this earth for at least a short while longer to try and do some good to it."

Leon put a reassuring hand on his father's arm. "Father was still quite weak when he returned," he said. "We left Sheffield for a few years to recover. While we were gone, my father learned about the terrible conditions in the mines, about how many people, how many *children,* were maimed or killed through the owners' careless greed. The mines here were owned by a business acquaintance of his, so my father purchased them, and immediately set about improving things."

"I wanted to find you and thank you," Mr. Black said, "but I could not recall precisely where you had lived, and I never saw you again before today."

"We moved away," Milcah said. "We only just returned."

"Father," Leon said, "surely then Miss Fox's request can be honoured and her land can be returned to her."

"Of course," Mr. Black said. "It only pains me to think it took this long for me to learn of it."

Milcah beamed. She felt like a huge weight had been lifted from her chest. "Thank you, Mr Black," she said.

"I'll have the deeds drawn up," Mr. Black said, "to ensure that it is official and nothing like this can happen again."

"Thank you, sir," her father said. He turned to Milcah. "I imagine Mr. Stentchen will be relieved, my dear, to not have you appearing on his doorstep every day. I think you were driving him quite mad."

But Milcah's smile wavered slightly, and she could not help glancing at Leon. She was incredibly relieved that the saga was over, of course, but she suddenly realised that she would have no reason to see or speak to Leon once the matter was settled. She had come to enjoy their verbal spars and his gentle smile. "Yes, papa," she said softly.

Leon noticed Milcah's suddenly downcast expression. "Miss Fox," he said. "Is something the matter? Don't tell me you will miss Mr. Stentchen."

"No," she said. "Not Mr. Stentchen. But I suppose I don't know what I will do with myself now."

"Perhaps I can help," Leon said. He turned to Milcah's father. "Now may not be the best time for it, but if I wait too long, I may lose my nerve. Mr. Fox, sir. I was hoping you might give me permission to ask your daughter to marry me."

Milcah swayed on the spot in shock. She gaped at Leon, and then at her father, trying to make his words make sense. Leon wanted to marry her? *Her,* Milcah Fox, who collected scraps of coal from around the mines as a child and never had enough ingredients to prepare a proper meal? Why would a rich, sophisticated man like Leon Fox wish to marry her?

She looked at his father, expecting Mr. Black to be disapproving, but he was beaming too, so she looked at her father instead, expecting some sign that she had misheard. But her father was smiling too. "I suppose that question is really up to Milcah," he said.

"Yes," Leon said. He took Milcah's hand with both of his. "Miss Fox. Milcah. I've told you before how much I value you, although I do not think you believed me. You are strong and brave and incredibly clever, and I would not want to spend my life with anybody else. Please tell me that you will consider marrying me."

"But—but I'm poor," she said. "I'm nobody. You could marry any girl you wanted—"

"And I wish to marry you," Leon said. "Nothing would make me happier. Please say yes."

She glanced at his father again, but he was still smiling. "My son's letter to me last night concerned two matters," he said. "First the issue of the land, but also the fact that he had found the woman he wished to marry, and he needed me to return as soon as possible to meet her. Considering our past, Miss Fox, I am inclined to think it fate. But of course, that is only if you are willing to accept my fool of a son as your husband."

"Yes," Milcah said. "I mean, he's not a fool, he's wonderful, but *yes*. That—that would make me very happy."

"Truly?" Leon asked, squeezing her hand. "Do you truly mean it?"

"Of course, I mean it," she said. "How could I not?"

"Sometimes," Leon admitted, "I got the feeling that you were not so fond of me."

"Oh, you're irritating enough," she said with a laugh. "And stubborn. Unstoppable when you have your mind fixed on something, and far too prone to argue with me. But," she added, her smile growing, "I have grown rather fond of you, nonetheless." She hoped that, despite her teasing, all her true, deep affection was clear in her voice, and from the way Leon's eyes sparkled, she knew that he had understood.

CHAPTER TWELVE

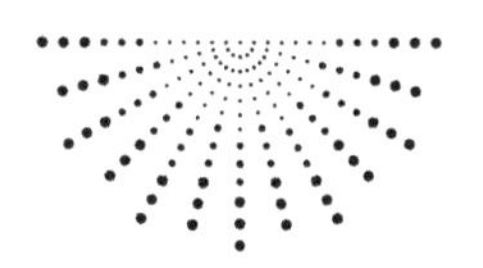

Milcah and Leon had a small wedding, with only their families present. Milcah purchased a new dress for the occasion, and she allowed Rachel and Leah to style her hair and pin her clothes *just so,* while they giggled and gossiped about what a handsome, kind, *rich* man Milcah would have as a husband.

The boys were thrilled to have Leon and his father join the family, as they had many more tall tales to share with Leon. They were even more delighted when they discovered that

Gerald Black had something of a talent for tall tales himself, and although Gerald once confided in Milcah that most of his stories came from books in his library, Milcah thought that the boys enjoyed Gerald's versions far more than if they had read the stories themselves.

Murray shed tears of pride for his daughter on her wedding day, and even Gerald seemed choked up at the sight of his son and his new wife, happy together. The couple travelled to Whitby for their honeymoon, enjoying the sea air, and then returned to a new house in Norton. Milcah could not abide the idea of servants—she had never been a lady of leisure, and she thought life would be unbearably boring if she became one—and she ran their little house herself, frequently cooking delicious feasts for the entire extended family.

Gerald and Leon both offered Murray and the other children a new house to live in, but all Murray wanted was to return to his lost family home. Both Murray and Milcah still refused to accept what they saw as charity, even from their in-laws, but Leon argued convincingly that his family owed the Foxes *something* for their use of their land for so long, and it was finally agreed that the Blacks would pay to get the land fit for the family again. With all the men working together, they added many improvements to the place, including a modern kitchen and a few extra bedrooms for the children.

Murray could no longer work the land, and it had never been very productive to begin with, so Milcah encouraged him to turn it into a garden for him to sit in and enjoy on the days when his limbs ached too much for him to walk far.

Leon occasionally travelled for work, but he always returned with gifts for Milcah and her siblings, and Milcah practiced her reading by looking through the many exciting recipe books that Leon collected for her from far-flung places across the north.

Scott and Russell took jobs in the mines, now that they were safer than ever, and although they were young, their confidence and charisma allowed them to progress quickly. Mr. Stentchen was still foreman, but Milcah imagined that one of her brothers would take the role once they were old enough and had proved themselves, and it made her happy to know that, despite their connection to the Black family, they were climbing in importance because of their own abilities. With the boys' income, the Fox family was soon able to buy plenty of wood for their fires and medicine for their father, even without the Blacks' assistance, and although Murray was never as strong as he once had been, his good days outnumbered his bad ones, and his family all delighted to see him healthier again.

The whole family took pride in the mines, especially remembering the horrific conditions they had seen there less than a decade before. Gerald Black provided housing for his workers, and medical care when needed, and never abandoned an employee when he became too old or sick to go down into the mines. The mines could never be completely without risk, but they did everything they could, and soon charitable folks and those campaigning for the rights of the poor were visiting and writing about the mines, presenting them as a shining example of what their new industrial society could be.

On a beautiful spring afternoon, about six months after the wedding, Milcah was working hard in the kitchen of her new house, preparing a special feast for her husband. She was recreating the first meal she ever served to Leon, during that family dinner that her sisters had so rashly invited him to, and she was determined to make it even more perfect than it had been before. She hummed happily to herself as she cooked, and she could not stop touching her stomach with joy and reverence on her face. She had life changing news for her husband when he returned home, and she could hardly wait another moment to tell him.

While she was cooking, she felt the ground rumble slightly beneath her feet. She paused for a moment, looking out of the window, but the world beyond seemed calm and still. Earthquakes were rare in the north of England, but they did happen, and a small rumble was nothing to be concerned about. The boys would be excited to talk about it, though, she thought with a smile.

But the hour grew later, and her husband did not return. This was not completely unheard of, as sometimes his work could delay him, but Milcah was eager to tell him the news, and she began to worry that he would not be home in time for the meal she had so lovingly prepared for the occasion.

Then she heard running footsteps outside. She turned and began to walk toward the entrance hall just as the front door flew open, and a panicked looking Russell ran inside.

"Russell!" Milcah said. Her heart dropped to her stomach. Russell's face was white, and he was covered in soot. "What's happened?"

"There was an explosion in the mines," Russell said. "Leon was in there, with a group of miners, and—"

Milcah was already running. She did not even pause to pull on shoes or grab her cloak as she raced down the hallway and out into the evening air.

"Where is he?" she asked her brother, as he ran beside her.

"We don't know," he said. "The entrance collapsed. They might be safe, but they could be buried in there. We don't know."

"He'll be safe," Milcah said. "He has to be."

Russell led her to the collapsed mine entrance. Gerald was already there, helping to dig through the rubble with many of the workers, including Scott, alongside him. Her father was there too, although he could not work himself, and as soon as he saw Milcah, he pulled her into his arms.

"What's happening?" Milcah asked. "Is there any news?"

"None yet," her father said. "Five men are missing, including your husband. Do not give up hope, Milcah. He is strong. He's a survivor."

Milcah nodded, fighting back tears. She wanted to believe him, but what did it matter if Leon was strong and a survivor, if an entire mine had fallen on his head?

Milcah paced in her bare feet while the men worked frantically to remove the rubble. At one point, unable to bear the waiting, she went up to the group and offered to haul rubble too, but the men refused her immediately, insisting that it still might not be safe. Milcah wanted to argue, but then she remembered the little one inside her, and she knew she could not take the risk.

Night fell, and the work continued. Milcah's sisters arrived with shoes and a cloak for her, and then they sat on a rock beside her, rubbing her hand occasionally in support but unable to speak. The men continued to work by the light of their lanterns, and although Milcah was terrified of the risk they were taking—what if there was a gas leak in the mines, and they sparked it with the flame?—she could not bear the idea that they might stop the search, any more than they seemed able to.

It must have been around midnight when the men gave out a cry. Milcah leapt to her feet at once and ran toward the sound, then stopped when she saw the men hauling two bodies away from the rubble. From where she stood, Milcah could see that neither of them was Leon, but when she saw their bleeding and broken bodies, she could not stop the gasp that burst out of her, shaking her whole body. If two of the five missing men were dead, what hope was there that Leon had survived? He was not the sort of man to put his own safety above others', especially his employees'. He would have died first.

Another woman let out a wail as she caught sight of the bodies, and she ran forward and grabbed one of the men's hands. Her cries cut straight to Milcah's heart, and Milcah knew instantly that that woman was experiencing the loss that she so feared.

Another sob burst out of her, and she collapsed to the ground. Tears ran down her face, and she was struggling to draw breath, when her father appeared beside her and put his arms around her.

"There is still hope, my dear," he said. Milcah shook her head. "Have faith, little one. Think on the past. The same God and grace that led me to Gerald in the river, the same God and grace that brought Leon to our family, is still watching over us all now, guiding us. Have faith.

Milcah nodded and took a deep breath, fighting back her tears. Panicking would help no one now. She needed to be strong and believe, for Leon's sake, and for the sake of the baby.

A few minutes later, she heard another shout, and looked up to see the rescuers helping two men stumble out of the rubble. Milcah jumped to her feet and ran forwards. Both survivors were filthy and bleeding, their clothes torn, but they were staggering out of the ruins on their own two feet, supported by their friends.

"My husband," she gasped to the two men. "Leon Black. Did you see him?" Four out of five men had been found. He alone remained trapped in the dark.

One of the survivors just shook his head, unable to look at Milcah, but the other looked at her with heartbroken eyes and replied in a rasping voice. "He saved us, miss," he said. "He wouldn't leave without us. He ran deeper into the mines, and then there was another collapse, more rocks and rubble... I'm sorry, miss, but I don't see much chance that he survived."

Milcah shook her head, unwilling to accept it. Her husband could not be dead. She pressed her hand to her stomach again, and behind the survivors, she saw Gerald's eyes widen, his face full of grief.

Milcah ran to the entrance of the mines, as though she might find her husband there. Gerald ran after her and put a comforting hand on her shoulder as she wept. Leon could not be gone. *Please,* she thought. Please don't let him be gone.

At that moment, she heard a faint cry, somewhere beyond the rubble. She stood up straighter, suddenly alert. "Did you hear that?" she asked.

No one responded. Then she heard the cry again, louder this time. It sounded like a muffled shout. And there was only one soul left in the mines now.

She ran right up to the collapsed rubble and fell to her knees, dragging the stones away with her bare hands.

"Leon!" she shouted. "Leon, are you there?"

The voice called again, sounding closer than before. Milcah frantically pulled stones away, and the other men joined her, moving at a desperate pace.

A few rocks slid, revealing a space behind them, an uncollapsed section of the mine. Milcah shouted, still sobbing, and this time she definitely heard Leon's pained voice crying back, "Milcah!"

A few more minutes of digging, and the space was large enough for a man to crawl through. A moment later, Leon staggered into view. His head was bleeding, and he was holding his arm against his body at a strange angle, but he was *alive*. Milcah leapt forward, tears streaming down her face, and threw her arms around him.

"Leon," she whispered. "Leon, you're alive." All around her, people were cheering, but Leon sobbed against her, wrapping his good arm around her. They stumbled the rest of the way out of the collapsed entrance, and then Leon fell to his knees, weeping.

"I could not save them, Milcah," he said. "I tried, but I failed."

"You did all you could," Milcah said, but Leon shook his head.

"They died in my arms," he said. "I tried to drag them to the surface, but they died, Milcah. And then I went back to help the others, but then more rock collapsed. I don't know—"

"They're alive," Milcah said. "They already got out. They said you saved them."

Leon shook his head. "I didn't do enough," he said.

"You got out," Milcah replied. "You came back to me."

"I wanted to give up hope," he admitted. "But when I thought of you, and of how God brought us together, I knew I had to have faith."

"I thought I had lost you," Milcah said. She held Leon tighter, and he cried into her shoulder, before slumping to the ground, unconscious.

CHAPTER THIRTEEN

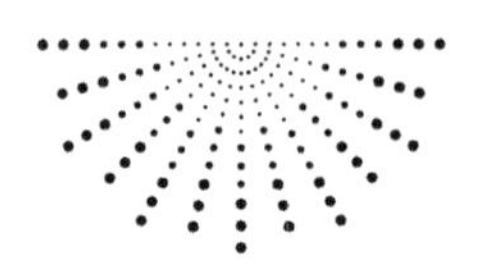

Gerald and Russell helped carry the unconscious Leon to Murray's home and laid his bruised body in bed, just as Murray laid Gerald in his bed to nurse him back to health all those years before.

Milcah bathed Leon's wounds while Scott ran to the doctor for his advice. The doctor, when he arrived, was a thin, severe-looking fellow with a wide walrus moustache. He looked over the unconscious Leon carefully, tutting occasionally, and then declared Leon's arm broken, but his physical health otherwise surprisingly undamaged by the event. Yet Leon did not awaken. The doctor diagnosed exhaustion as the cause of his unconsciousness, exhaustion of both the body and the soul, and declared that while he saw no reason why the man should not recover fully, the spirit could have a strange influence on recovery, and the loss of his men, more than the injuries he himself suffered, might pose a threat to his health.

"Complete rest," the doctor prescribed, "and quiet. Beyond repairing his physical injuries, that is all the advice that I can offer."

The doctor set and splinted Leon's arm, and Leon barely stirred during the painful procedure. The doctor then stitched up the wound on Leon's head, and bid Milcah and the family a solid goodbye, with a promise to return upon the morrow.

Milcah was exhausted by the evening's ordeal, but she could not bear to sleep. She sat by Leon's bedside, holding his hand tightly in both of hers, and praying for him to wake.

All night, he did not stir. Milcah stayed by his side, thinking of the past that they had shared, and the bright future that she had dreamed for them together. She thought of their son or daughter, still so very small, and how much they would need their papa to love and care for them and teach them about life and about how a good person should be.

When the doctor returned, he admonished Milcah for not resting herself, and insisted that someone else take over Leon's care. Milcah tried to protest, but Gerald and Murray both agreed, and as soon as Milcah allowed herself to lie down for a moment, the exhaustion overtook her, and she fell asleep.

When she awoke, she heard Gerald and her father talking quietly together.

"Has she told you about the baby?" Gerald asked.

"Not with words," her father replied, "but I see it in how she carries herself."

"All this stress cannot be good for her," Gerald said, "or for the child."

"Milcah will not rest while Leon is unwell," her father said. "It is not in her nature."

Milcah pretended to be asleep until the topic of conversation ended and Gerald left to care for his son again, and then rose. One look at her father's face told her that Leon's condition had not changed.

Her father wrapped his arms around her, and she squeezed back as hard as she could. She desperately wished, for just a moment, to be small again, small enough to sit on her father's lap and trust him to be able to solve all the problems in the world. Small enough to believe that only good things happened to good people, and that nothing could take her family away.

"I know, my love," her father said, as she cried into his shoulder. "I know."

Milcah closed her eyes tightly, fighting back tears, and sent out another desperate prayer.

Just this one, she thought, let goodness be rewarded. Let Leon's generous, charitable spirit, which saved the lives of two men and attempted to save two more, not lead to his child growing up without a father.

In the other room, Gerald gasped. Milcah stepped back from her father's embrace, turning to the doorway, as Gerald spoke. He was sobbing. "Lord, thank you," he said. "You have granted me my son back from the edge of death, not once now, but twice."

Milcah hurried to the door. As she did so, she heard Gerald speak again. "God has given me my child back again, and another dear child to bring double joy to my heart."

Milcah stepped into the room. Her husband was lying on the bed, his eyes open, looking up at his father in confusion. Gerald knelt by the side of the bed, sobbing. As soon as Milcah entered the room, Leon's gaze shifted to her. "Milcah?" he rasped. He reached out for her hand.

Milcah walked slowly forward, unable to stop the gentle smile spreading across her face as she took Leon's hand and pressed it gently against her stomach. He looked up at her with wide-eyed wonder, and Milcah nodded, tears streaming down her face.

THANK YOU FOR CHOOSING A PUREREAD BOOK!

We hope you enjoyed the story, and as a way to thank you for choosing PureRead we'd like to send you this free book, and other fun reader rewards…

Click here for your free copy of Whitechapel Waif

PureRead.com/victorian

Thanks again for reading.
See you soon!

HAVE YOU READ?

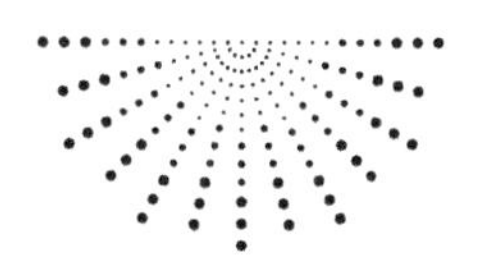

THE MILL DAUGHTER'S COURAGE?

Now that you have read 'The Coal Scavenger's Daughter' why not continue with another hope-filled Victorian Romance.

The resilient faith you have witnessed in Milcah's story is reflected in another PureRead tale called *The Mill Daughter's Courage* - the story of an English mill girl, Daisy Barlow.

The story begins amidst the shadows and perils of a foreboding

industrial mill. Yet here amidst the gloom, Daisy Barlow discovers pockets of happiness in her mother, Vera, and her twin sister, Janet – until tragedy strikes...

The untimely death of her beloved sister and the soul-crushing grief of her mother push Daisy to an agonizing juncture – one that leaves her all alone to **fend for herself against seemingly insurmountable odds**. But Daisy is not a quitter!

Far from defeated, her spirit remains unyielding, fuelled by the unwavering belief in her mother's eventual recovery and the promise of a brighter future. Surely her sister's death was not in vain.

Will sweet Daisy survive this cruel world to find her Happily Ever After?

For your enjoyment here are the first chapters of her story...

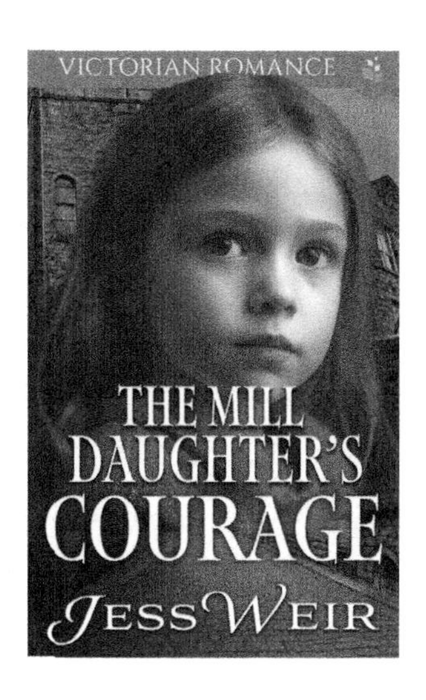

Daisy Barlow sneezed so loudly that it could almost be heard over the dreadful din of the machinery. Having spent half her young life working in the mill, it was a wonder that Daisy's nose was still so sensitive to the tiny flying particles of cotton lint.

Janet, who was under one of the machines hastily tying the two ends of a snapped thread, slid out and stood upright, grinning like a fool and mimicking the motion of a sneeze before pretending to cover her ears against the sound.

Daisy laughed and shook her head. Her twin sister always made her laugh. However bad the day was, Janet Barlow could see some good in it, or if not the good, then at least a little humour. Daisy didn't know how other children managed the long days at the mill without a twin of their own to take the edge off things.

Daisy's attention quickly returned to her work. Her mother, Vera, had seen her beloved girls out of the corner of her eye and quickly shook her head from side to side. Daisy knew her mother was just worried that Mr Baker would see and reprimand the girls or, worse still, dock their already meagre wages. And, of course, there was the ever-present threat of being reported to Mr Wainwright for misbehaving. He was famous for his short temper and penchant for the arbitrary dismissal of a mill worker without so much as a minute's hearing.

Turning to look at her mother, Daisy gave her a tiny nod to put her mind at rest and turned her eyes back to the loom. In return, Vera smiled at her daughter, so briefly that nobody could have accused her of not getting on with her work. Over the years, the family of three had developed their own system of silent communication in a world which was anything but.

Daisy turned her attention back to the shuttle quill she was loading with thread. She needed to be fast for Mr Baker didn't like the little things taking too much time. *Time was money,* that's what Mr Baker always said. Of course, for Daisy and her mother and sister, *time* was a *pittance,* for their pay barely kept them alive.

Daisy could see that Janet had already moved on from her amusement and was fully absorbed in wiping down. As far as Daisy could tell, it was just about the worst job in the entire mill. The worker, usually the younger children, would have to dart between the two heaviest parts of the power loom to wipe it down. In its practice, it wasn't any better or worse than many other jobs in the mill. To Daisy, however, the noise was horrendous. It was nothing compared to the inattentiveness of the man holding the carriage of the loom back on its brakes. Add in the sheer weight of the loom carriages —it made the whole thing more life-threatening.

Although she gave every appearance of working on her own task, Daisy watched the wiping down like a hawk when Janet was the child sent in to do it. She wanted to be ready to pull on the brakes herself if the man in charge of them let them go too quickly.

The problem was that Janet was small. They were both thirteen years old, but Daisy was tall, and Janet was short and slight, like a tiny fairy. She was still able to take the same awful tasks that were reserved for children. At thirteen, Daisy and Janet were hardly that. No, children were five, six or at the most seven. At thirteen, childhood was long gone, if it had ever truly been there in the first place.

As she wound the thread back onto the shuttle, Daisy felt every nerve ending standing to attention. She moved a little to her right, closer to David Langley, the man standing at the brake lever. With her eyes darting back and forth between her sister and David, Daisy felt the dreadful sense of anxiety which seemed to sweep over her so many times in her working day. It was so common that it had come to feel like a perpetual state.

It was nearing the end of the day. A day which had begun sixteen hours before. It was the time of day, often referred to by the little ones as *the death time*. It was a disturbingly accurate description, for the last two hours of the working day were the hours in which most of the accidents happened. People who had worked for so many hours were exhausted enough, without the ceaseless noise of the machinery making it even harder to concentrate.

Shuttles banged from side to side, the engines roared, and the very walls of the mill seemed almost to shake. There was no escape from the din, and it was debilitating. All in all, *the death time* should have come as no surprise to anybody. Who could possibly concentrate as well in the *death time* as they had first thing in the morning after a little rest and a little quiet?

When Janet slid out from beneath the mule of the machine, Daisy breathed a sigh of relief. David let go of the brakes immediately, as he always did. Janet was barely clear of the loom when the carriage slid back with a bang loud enough to compete with so many other dreadful sounds. Langley always let go of the brakes like that. It was ingrained into them all that the machines should not be idle for long. When the machines stopped, the pay stopped. David Langley was in no better position than the Barlow family, and she could understand a poor man's desire to get the machine going straight away. Perhaps, he might have been a little less hasty had the person doing the wiping down been his own daughter or sister.

With her nerves shredded, Daisy knew that the final hour of the working day couldn't pass by fast enough. She needed to be out of the noise and out of danger, letting go of the fear for a few hours until morning rolled around once more.

~

Janet was chattering to her as the girls and their mother got ready for the short journey home. It was a relief to get a little cool air, having suffered the tremendous heat of the mill for so many hours.

"I thought today would never end!" Janet said brightly, shouting instead of speaking, as so many mill workers did as they readjusted to the world outside of the unspeakable noise.

"Me too. I've almost sneezed my brains clean out today." Daisy was always ready to join in a little banter and have her beloved twin raise her spirits on the way home.

"Almost?" Janet was still loud, still adjusting. "They came right out, I saw them. They flew out of your nose and landed in Mr Baker's deep pockets!"

"Janet!" their mother hissed, looking over her shoulder.

"He's not here, is he, Mama? He's not out here with those of us of the bare-foot brigade searching for the right clogs to walk home in." Janet was giggling.

"Maybe he isn't here, my love, but there are them as would run to him and tell him if they thought it would do them some benefit. And think of Mr Wainwright! He's as like to throw out an entire family as throw out just one noisy girl, isn't he? Then where shall we be?" She sobered her voice. "And what would God think of us? Talking about another rudely behind their backs. It isn't the Christian or the kind thing to do, no matter how mean Mr Wainwright may get,"

"Sorry, Mama," Janet was quiet now, her pretty face full of heartfelt apology as she eased her bare feet into her clogs.

Daisy smiled, Janet was the light of her life, but she knew their mother was right. They must always be careful when they spoke. Even at the end of the day when a myriad of workers, all of whom had worked barefoot in the mill room to avoid sparks from their clog irons igniting the snow-like cotton dust which covered the floors, were re-shooing themselves for the walk home.

Daisy wrapped her shawl around herself tightly, making her way to the open door of the mill and out into the cool evening air. Working in the almost crippling heat and stifled recirculated air of the mill was almost like working in another country. The outside air always felt like something of a shock at the end of the working day, even if it was a blessed relief to draw a breath which didn't fill the lungs with soft cotton dust.

"What shall we have for our tea tonight?" Janet asked, chattering happily as they walked home, their clogs tapping a rhythmic beat as they went. "Shall we have venison?" she went on, laughing and completely recovered from their mother's telling-off.

"Or shall we have salmon and trout?" Daisy played along, always feeling a burst of relief at this time every day that the three of them had made it out of the mill for another day alive and with their full complement of fingers.

"Or shall we keep a hold of the real world and just eat the potato and cabbage stew we've been heating and re-heating all week long?" Vera stated with a sigh. She did, however, look at her girls and smile.

"Aye, let's do that! You can't beat cabbage at the end of a long day." Janet was as high-spirited at night as she was first thing in the morning.

“You’ve a fair humour on you, child, I’ll give you that, but you tire me right enough,” Vera said and laughed.

“Just think, in three days it will be Sunday. Nothing to do but go to church. No sounds but the birdsong to replace the looms.” Daisy was getting in the spirit of things.

“Not you too, Daisy!” Vera said and chuckled. “Not my sensible child! We’ve cleaning to be doing on Sunday as you very well know. That shameless landlord will be poking his beak into things, looking for some excuse to put the rent up again. No, my girl, we’ll need to have the floor scrubbed and the mattresses tidied away in their corners. As the saying goes, there’s no rest for the wicked.”

“Then we must truly be the most wicked three females on earth, Mama, for there really is never a moment of rest,” Daisy said and began to feel deflated.

"That won't help, my little chick. Try to stay above it all like your sister does. It won't do to dwell."

It won't do to dwell was a phrase their mother had used day in, day out since their father had left them six years before when the twins were just seven. Vera had been right, of course, it really didn't do to dwell. There wasn't time to dwell, not even for the tiny girls who had been forced to work in the mill alongside their mother just to make ends meet.

Perhaps if their father had stayed, Janet wouldn't have to crawl between the loom carriage and the roller beam every day. Perhaps Daisy wouldn't have to swallow down the ball of fear in her throat each time. But Tom Barlow had gone, and he wasn't coming back. He'd left Burnley with his lover and had moved to goodness-knew-where to live in sin with her. Perhaps they had moved far enough away that they might pretend to be man and wife. Either way, Daisy Barlow would never,

ever forgive him. Mother taught forgiveness, and how everyone deserved it, "just as Jesus forgave us all" she would say – but Daisy didn't think a father who abandoned his family deserved forgiveness at all.

"Don't you think it's funny that Mr Baker is called Mr Baker, but he's not a baker, he works in a mill?" Janet said, breaking Daisy out of her dark train of thought. "And that Mr Wainwright is called Mr Wainwright, but he isn't a wainwright, but the man who owns the mill. I suppose a relation of his must have been a wainwright at some time, don't you think, Mama?"

"I think you need to do less thinking, lass, if that's the best you can come up with!" Vera said, and they all laughed. "Come on, girls, let's get home!"

Janet stopped suddenly, and stood upright as if in shock. "I think we shall have the salmon and trout on Tuesday in three weeks! For that is a special day!"

Daisy giggled, understanding her sister's joke.

Vera smiled. "And why is that day so special?"

Daisy's eyes seemed to twinkle even brighter than usual. "Because that Tuesday is our birthday!"

"Have you not swept that lot up yet, Janet?" Vera Barlow asked with mild exasperation.

"Mama, I swept it up twice already. I don't know where it all comes from. That ceiling has been peeling for so long now that it's a wonder we're not just looking up at the clear sky!"

"Come on, Janet, let me sweep for a while," Daisy said and smiled at her sister as she took the broom. "She's right though, Mama, I remember this ceiling being in a dreadful state when we first came here after Father... well... when we first came here."

"Six years of peeling, day in, day out. It must be a miracle of some kind that it hasn't peeled itself completely away." Janet sat on an upturned bucket in the middle of the room, the bucket she was to fill with water from the pump outside to wash the bare wooden floorboards of their one-room home in the Burnley slums.

"It'd be a bigger miracle if Joe Hamill had the place painted just once. And the wooden window frames are so rotten that as much cold air flies through this room when the windows are closed as when they are open. He really *is* a shameless charlatan, Mama," Daisy said, already having half the room swept.

"Be that as it may, there isn't a right lot we can do about it, Daisy. I don't know what sort of places you think the three of us can afford on our money." Sometimes Vera was just down, struggling beneath the weight of so much responsibility and hopelessness. "This is as good as our sort get."

"Mama, I know you don't mean that. It might be all we get, but it's not what we deserve. Joe Hamill might have clawed his way to own a rundown building or two, but he soon forgot where he came from, didn't he? He soon learned, like them rich ones do, that the best way of making money is either out of our pockets or off our backs. If the ceiling is peeling away to nothing, Mama, it's Joe Hamill's shame, not ours." Still sweeping, Daisy turned to look over her shoulder and smile at her mother. "The three of us do everything we can in this life, don't we?"

"That we do, my little chick. That we do," Vera said and smiled back, making Daisy feel relieved.

By the time the Barlow family had paid their rent every week, there was very little left for anything else. The slums were the cheapest possible rent, but that rent was still far too high for what they received. It was a trap that the working poor fell into. A trap set by those who knew their circumstances well and had already discovered the best ways to profit by those circumstances. To keep a roof over their head, a poor family had nowhere else to go but the slums. That being the case, the landlord was free to allow the housing to fall into any state of disrepair he chose. Always reminding his tenants that if they were not happy, they might leave at any time. Always knowing that they couldn't afford to be anywhere better.

Daisy wasn't a vengeful girl, but she certainly spent a good part of her day hoping that the people who had done the worst in this life, taken advantage of others, made money from their plight, would suffer for it one day as she and her kind had suffered. And it *was* suffering to live in such a place, especially for a girl who could remember what life was like before her father had disappeared.

They'd never been wealthy, far from it, but they'd rented a tiny two up two down terraced house in a slightly cleaner part of Burnley. Knowing how to read and write, Tom Barlow had occasionally found himself in jobs which paid a little better than the rest. It certainly wasn't enough for luxuries, but at least his wife and daughters had a little more by way of clothing than one dress for the week and one for Sundays. When he had still been at home, they'd all had a bonnet. However, years of wear and growing had seen them all bonnet-less for some time now.

Their room was on the ground floor of a two-story brick-built house. The walls had creeping mould where the damp from the outside made its way through the gaps and rotten woodwork after years of neglect. Even though it never seemed to go anywhere, Daisy spent a good part of every Sunday with a brush and a pail of hot water trying to get rid of it.

There was a fireplace in the room, over which the family cooked their meagre meals. There was a rail affixed to the chimney breast which held the family's only two pans and one spoon for stirring. There was an iron rail, which ended in a flat plate, set inside the fireplace, somewhere to set down a pan for cooking.

Their beds were no better than narrow mattresses on the floor, mattresses they'd had so long that Daisy couldn't even remember how and where they had acquired them, she only knew that they had never been brand-new to the family. No doubt countless people had slept on them before they'd made their way into the Barlow family's small abode.

They left the mattresses on the floor all week long, made up ready for them to crawl into after a long day's work. However, on Sundays, the mattresses were heaved up on their end, leaned against a wall, and covered with a sheet. Sunday was a day when Joe Hamill might appear at any moment, and Vera not only wanted to avoid him declaring the place to be a mess and adding a shilling to the rent, but she had her own pride too. Their home might not have been much, but she was determined to keep it clean and decent.

In fact, Vera was so determined that there was only a pot to be used in emergencies. Otherwise, she and her daughters wandered out of the back of the house, day or night, to the shared privy at the far end of the row. Daisy hated the shared privy. Nobody ever seemed to take responsibility for keeping it clean, and as a result, it was an awful place.

"Have you not swept that lot up yet, Daisy?" Janet asked, parroting her mother's earlier words and grinning like a court jester.

"I never knew anybody as cheeky as you!" Daisy said, trying to sound stern but unable to keep her amusement out of her voice, much less her face.

"What would life be like if I wasn't around to be cheeky anymore? Dull, that's what!" Janet said and got to her feet, picking up the bucket she'd been sitting on and heading out of the door to fill it at the pump.

As Daisy swept up the last curls of peeled paint, she looked over at her mother. They smiled at one another; they knew that life was made better by Janet and her cheeky ways.

~

It was late on Wednesday, and Daisy could hardly believe that they still had three full sixteen-hour days of work to do before Sunday came around again. Why was it that Sunday passed by so quickly and the rest of the week dragged along in noise and dust and worry?

"Daisy," Mr Baker had come up beside her and bellowed in her ear, trying to make himself heard over the machinery. "Go across to the back loom, the thread keeps snapping. I know your hands aren't tiny, but you're nimble enough. But mind you concentrate; I don't want to have to shut off the machine if you lose a finger in there."

Daisy stared at him for a moment before a gentle shove propelled her in the right direction. She didn't want to be on the other side of the mill, she always liked to have her mother and sister close enough to see. However, Mr Baker, the man who managed the day-to-day running of the mill for Mr Wainwright, was not a man to be argued with. So, Daisy hurried through the room, her bare feet kicking up the soft, fluffy cotton dust as she went.

The other loom really did need looking at and looking at properly. The thread was snapping every few minutes, and there was clearly either a problem with the bobbins or the gap settings on the loom itself. Either way, if she simply kept re-tying the threads, somebody would later be complaining about having to trim the loose ones off the fabric, possibly even Mr Baker himself.

After almost half an hour of tying the threads, the decision was made to shut down the loom and fix the problem. Daisy could see the disappointment on so many faces, none of them keen to take the drop in pay that inevitably resulted from one of the looms going down, whether it was their fault or not.

It was time for Daisy to get out of the way and Mr Baker, without words, pointed her back across to her original work of making sure that the shuttles flew through the threads easily on each pass. Her mother was doing the same job a few feet away from her, her focus fully absorbed. As Daisy resumed her own work, she scanned the room for any sign of Janet.

Not seeing her anywhere, she felt that little sense of panic she always felt. This time, however, there was a sudden prickling at the back of her neck, a sense of dreadful foreboding. Taking her eyes off her own work entirely, Daisy realised that one of the looms had been opened, its carriage drawn out and held back on brakes. No doubt Janet, small and nimble, was inside, crouched down, wiping away the dust which choked the looms so regularly.

As always, Daisy fixed her attention on David Langley. She could see that the man regularly looked over his shoulder at the unfolding drama of the dormant loom at the back of the room. With his hand on the brake lever, Daisy held her breath. Why couldn't the man just concentrate on what he was doing, instead of worrying what the closed loom was going to do to his pay packet?

With the greatest sense that something was about to go wrong, Daisy felt a horrible feeling in the pit of her stomach. Even though nothing had yet happened, she had a sense that it was already too late. Daisy left her post and began to cross to where David was. She crouched down as she made her way, looking for any sign of Janet and seeing her similarly crouched just exactly where she expected to see her; between the carriage and the roller beam.

As if it was always going to happen, the distracted David Langley, likely as bone-tired as the rest of them and in need of a break, absentmindedly pushed at the brake lever. Daisy opened her mouth to scream, her arms spread wide as she tried to get the man's attention. However, her scream died in the noise of the room, and she knew that it was already too late the moment he had pushed the brake lever.

The carriage flew back instantly, that horrible bang as it settled into place once more. Daisy dropped to the floor, scrabbling on her hands and knees, trying to find her sister. Perhaps the only saving grace, when she did find her, was to know that it would have been quick. Janet wouldn't have lingered.

Crushed between the back of the loom carriage and the immovable roller beam, Janet Barlow's head lolled to one side, her chest and shoulders flattened. The heavy machinery pinned her there in such a position, such a garish, awful position, that Daisy knew she would never forget it for the rest of her life.

Daisy, on her hands and knees, was violently sick. Bit by bit, the room began to fall silent.

There was a commotion behind her, all around her the men were powering down the looms. Bare feet were running backwards and forwards in a blind panic. It was the first time in the six years that Daisy had worked in the mill that the machines had all been powered down at once, and it seemed that the sudden silence caused a great pressure inside her ears, inside her head.

Suddenly realising that there was somebody at her side, Daisy tried to turn to look, but couldn't take her eyes off her sister. Her beloved twin sister; the other half of her. The funny half, the light-hearted half, the tiny and most precious half.

It was only when she heard her mother's heartbroken screams that she realised that it was *she* crouched down by her side, *she* who was staring across at the broken, lifeless body of the daughter she couldn't reach...

How will Daisy survive without her beloved twin sister to cheer her days? Will her mother's grief consume all that is good and pure leaving nothing but devastation?

Discover all in the compelling new book by Jess Weir, The Mill Daughter's Courage.

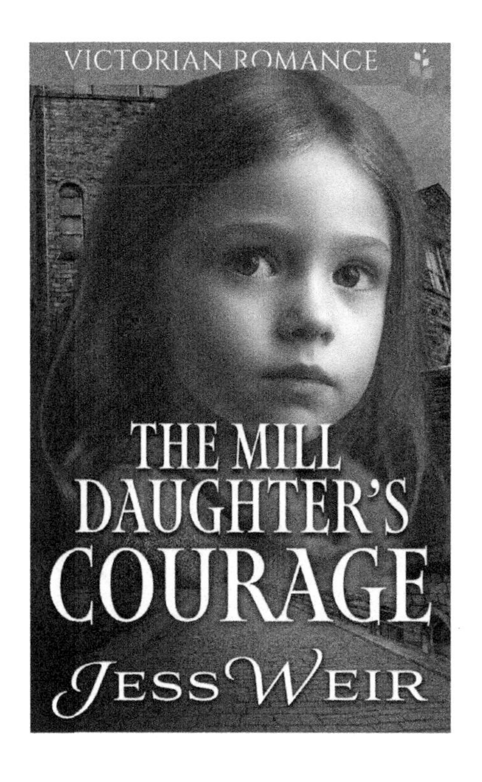

Start Reading Now

LOVE VICTORIAN ROMANCE?

If you enjoyed this story why not continue straight away with other books in our PureRead Victorian Romance library?

Orphan Christmas Miracle

An Orphan's Escape

The Lowly Maiden's Loyalty

Ruby of the Slums

The Dancing Orphan's Second Chance

Cotton Girl Orphan & The Stolen Man

Victorian Slum Girl's Dream

The Lost Orphan of Cheapside

Dora's Workhouse Child

Saltwick River Orphan

Workhouse Girl and The Veiled Lady

OUR GIFT TO YOU

AS A WAY TO SAY THANK YOU WE WOULD LOVE TO SEND YOU THIS BEAUTIFUL STORY FREE OF CHARGE.

Our Reader List is 100% FREE

Click here for your free copy of Whitechapel Waif

PureRead.com/victorian

At PureRead we publish books you can trust. Great tales without smut or swearing, but with all of the mystery and romance you expect from a great story.

Be the first to know when we release new books, take part in our fun competitions, and get surprise free books in your inbox by signing up to our Reader list.

As a thank you you'll receive an exclusive copy of Whitechapel Waif - a beautiful book available only to our subscribers...

Click here for your free copy of Whitechapel Waif

PureRead.com/victorian

Printed in Great Britain
by Amazon

32496662R00121